Praise for Penel
AND *The Mean*

"She is, isn't she, the best." —**A. S. Byatt**

"Outstanding . . . brims with comedy, horror and satire . . . If Edgar Allan Poe were alive today, he could surely have done no better." —*San Francisco Chronicle*

"Fitzgerald's posthumous—and only—story collection serves as an elegiac gift to dedicated fans of her award-winning novels and a tantalizing introduction for new readers . . . *The Means of Escape* sparkles with her trademark appreciation of life's fine absurdities." —*Entertainment Weekly*

"Warm and wry, her writing is as economical as it is perfect . . . always a pleasure." —*Washington Post*

"The droplet Fitzgerald furnishes is a world, not the world as we know it but as she incites us to suspect it. She turns us into microscopes: we see not only her characters' thoughts, purposes and actions but the gallivanting, subvisible antibodies that disarrange them." —*New York Times*

"[Fitzgerald is] among the two or three best novelists in England today . . . The breadth of her knowledge, the lucidity of her intelligence and the quirkiness of her characters provide the satisfaction of a nineteenth-century novel, yet there is nothing musty or old-fashioned about any of her books . . . Hers is a tone of understated amusement in the face of human struggle, a dry chuckle that is the preferred alternative to tears. She writes sentences that jot forward and back, seeking with inflection and qualifier to encapsulate an observation; as in a Matisse drawing, what is left out is as crucial as what is set down." — *New York Times Magazine*

"Where some writers like to build effects slowly, Fitzgerald prefers a quicksilver economy. Vivid, elegant, astonishing."
— *Washington Post Book World*

"Strange, whimsical, sometimes gothic or bizarre, these tales demonstrate Fitzgerald's cool and civilized wit and the merciless eye she casts on worldly pretensions . . . Crisp, with the economical suggestiveness of poetry, these stories will be treasured by Fitzgerald's readers."
— *Publishers Weekly*, **starred review**

"Her dry, shrewd, sympathetic, and sharply economical books are almost disreputably enjoyable. Fugitive scraps of insight and information, like single brushstrokes of vivid and true colors, convey much more reality than any amount of impasto description and research."
— *New York Times Book Review*

"No writer is more engaging than Penelope Fitzgerald."
— **Anita Brookner**, *Spectator*

Books by Penelope Fitzgerald

Fiction

The Golden Child
The Bookshop
Offshore
Human Voices
At Freddie's
Innocence
The Beginning of Spring
The Gate of Angels
The Blue Flower
The Means of Escape

Nonfiction

Edward Burne-Jones
The Knox Brothers
Charlotte Mew and Her Friends

THE MEANS
of
ESCAPE

———◉———

Penelope Fitzgerald

A Mariner Book
HOUGHTON MIFFLIN COMPANY
BOSTON · NEW YORK

CONTENTS

INTRODUCTION

I KNEW Penelope Fitzgerald—never well—for a long time. We taught together in the 1960s at a very English institution called the Westminster Tutors, which prepared seventeen-year-olds for the entrance exams, now abolished, to Oxford and Cambridge Universities. I was very young and harassed in those days, with two small children. I met Penelope over coffee between tutorials from time to time. Looking back, I see that the teaching suited both of us, concentrating as it did on the very clever and the very willing, taught in groups of two or three. Penelope later reproduced some of the atmosphere of that eccentric place—including its smell—in *At Freddie's,* in which the formidable Miss Freeston, who ran the Tutors, has become Freddie, the principal of a school for child actors. It would not have occurred to me at the time that Penelope might do anything of the kind—and possibly not to her, either. The portrait of Freddie is both wicked and just, attentive and judging. What I registered about Penelope at the time was an interest in precision. I remember remarking casually that I had corrected a student for writing about the "protagonists" of a drama. My mother, I said, had told me that the word should never be used in the plural. "Why?" asked Penelope. Because it came from the Greek, I said, and the protagonist in Greek drama was the leading actor — there was only one — and the second actor was called the deuteragonist. It was like "unique," which is an adjective you shouldn't qualify with "very" or "rather" because a thing either is unique or it isn't. These distinctions pleased Penelope, who liked exactness where it was possible. For the next thirty years, when we met, she reminded me of this conversation.

The other thing I remember about Penelope was her understanding of, and fear for, very intelligent children. Children in her fiction are — as real children are — wiser and more resourceful than fragile adults. Consider the families in both *Offshore* and *Innocence,* as well as Bernhard in *The Blue Flower* and the perfectionist boy actor in *At Freddie's.* She taught my daughter at the Tutors long after I had left, and told me rather pointedly that I did not seem to realize that my daughter had "a touch of genius." Since I had said nothing about that, and would have felt it wrong to boast, I felt harshly judged. She appeared mild and retiring, and could be suddenly sharp and incisive. I was also grateful that she had noticed my daughter. When, later, I read her account of her family—from which she scrupulously almost excludes herself, recording her own birth simply as "a grandchild"—I understood better her own relationship to pure brilliance and eccentricity, the way she was at home with intelligence and careful about those in whom it might not be cherished or recognized. She was a brilliant student herself, who became a good biographer and a good teacher. She discovered her own genius as a novelist, I feel, as she went along, rising apparently effortlessly to the stories and forms provided by her own intelligence. Another occasion when I felt she had judged me myself for falling short was when she told me that no one had noticed that *Human Voices* turned on a German poem by Heine. She felt that I might "write something about it so that people would understand." But at that stage I did not understand it myself. I thought she was a good comic English novelist who had read Muriel Spark well. It was only when I read the late, remote novels about other times and places that I came to be able to take on the moral ferocity, the elegance of mind, the bleakness and generosity of her vision. People in England still tended to see her as a good English biographer— of Burne-Jones, of the eccentric Charlotte Mew, who appealed to students of women's writing—who happened to write novels. Her masterpiece as a biographer seems to me to be her composite biography of her father and his brothers, *The Knox Brothers*. It is a portrait of English intelligence, religion, oddity, pigheadedness, and wisdom, written with a completely self-effacing directness and unobtrusive wit. She was the granddaughter of a bishop, the niece of two very different priests, and, like her family, religious. Hermione Lee, interviewing her for *New Writing*, pressed her on her feminism, her political beliefs. Penelope corrected her. She hoped her work reflected her *spiritual* life.

I now think she was one of the best novelists of my lifetime. What follows is based on an article I wrote for the *Threepenny Review* in San Francisco at a time when many of her novels were out of print in the States. The success of *The Blue Flower,* for which she won the National Book Award — the first non-American to do so — changed that. I am glad she must have known, before she died, that readers were beginning to understand her full subtlety and mastery. She would never have put herself forward, but she knew how good she was.

Penelope Fitzgerald wrote discreet, brief, perfect tales. Her first novel was published in 1977 when she was already over sixty. She won the Booker Prize in 1979 for *Offshore,* a comedy with an edge about a family barely surviving on a houseboat on the Thames. Her early novels are English — kindly studies of the endless absurdity of human behavior, seen simultaneously with an unwavering moral gaze. She was interested in traditional forms — the plotted detective story, the supernatural tale. In 1986, with *Innocence,* she began to write about other countries — Italy, Russia, Germany — and other centuries. This looking outward from English manners was in the air at the time, and there has been a flowering of historically and geographically various fiction in Britain. But Fitzgerald's later novels are quite extraordinarily good. They made me at least reread the earlier ones with closer attention, consider the delicious sentences, come to the conclusion that Fitzgerald was Jane Austen's nearest heir for precision and invention. But she has other qualities, qualities I think of as European and metaphysical. She has what Henry James called "the imagination of disaster." She can make a reader helpless with inordinate private laughter. (I will give examples.) She is also one of those writers whose sentences, however brief, are recognizable as hers and no one else's, although they are classically elegant and unfussy.

Consider the description of the BBC during the Second World War in *Human Voices*. "Broadcasting House was in fact dedicated to the strangest project of the war, or of any war, that is, telling the truth." It goes on "Without prompting, the BBC had decided that truth was more important than consolation, and in the long run would be more effective." The novel is a wonderful combination of deadpan English comedy and surreal farce, from the death in the studio of a French general whose post-Dunkirk message turns out to be a passionate plea to the English to surrender to Hitler immediately, to the recording, for a program called "Lest We Forget Our Englishry," of "six hundred bands of creaking. To be accurate some are a mixture of squeaking and creaking."

"They're all from the parish church of Hither Lickington," Sam explained eagerly. "It was recommended to us by Religious Broadcasting. What you're hearing is the hinges of the door and the door itself opening and shutting as the old women come in one by one with the stuff for the Harvest Festival. The quality's superb, particularly on the last fifty-three bands or so."

Sam is Director of Recorded Programmes, one of Fitzgerald's fatally dangerous narrow-minded innocents, a technical perfectionist who flirts plaintively and indifferently with a seraglio of assistants. His obsession is part of what makes up the awkwardly powerful survival of the BBC. He is loved by an assistant (with perfect pitch) from Birmingham called Annie Asra. Fitzgerald named this person, also singleminded, for a poem, "Der Asra," by Heine. The Asra are a tribe of slaves *"welche sterben, wenn sie lieben"* (who die when they love). German Romantic orientalism is an odd component of so very English a novel, and Fitzgerald's surprise that no one noticed the reference was perhaps innocently unrealistic. But it is also a pointer to un-English preoccupations.

Innocence (1986) opens with a delicious and chilling account of a sixteenth-century Italian noble family, the Ridolfi, who were midgets. The cosseted and innocent midget daughter has a dwarf companion who suddenly grows to a normal height. To the midget mistress this is a monstrous misfortune. After much kind reflection she decides it would be best to put out the other girl's eyes and cut off her legs at the knees, so that she would "never know the increasing difference between her and the rest of the world."

This tale resonates through the novel about the fortunes of a modern Ridolfi (of normal height), Chiara, in the 1950s, who falls in love at first sight (at the opera) with a handsome doctor of southern socialist stock, with whom she has nothing in common except love and a singlemindedness reminiscent of Annie Asra in wartime London. Both Chiara and her Salvatore are, in their innocence, dangerous to themselves and others; both are also hopeful and lovable. What is remarkable about this tale (of only 220 pages) is the completeness of its Italianness, political, religious, moral, and physical. There is a monsignor, an old comrade, a dying lady who founded a charity, a farming cousin who finds words unnecessary; there are political and family intrigues and a curious and purely Italian mixture of passion and heartlessness. There is a moving scene with an ancient haute couture designer; there is a suddenly appalling brief scene where the child Salvatore is taken to see the dying politician Gramsci in the hospital, and finds not socialist inspiration but a medical vocation in the horror of his decay. There is a huge, ungainly English aristocratic friend of the delicate Chiara who lumbers emotionally and forcefully through the story. It is an exquisite mosaic where every tiny piece is part of an intrigue and a world, olives and lemons, clothes and manners. Tragedy is possible, and farce is omnipresent, both belied by the light, decorous storytelling. Every time I reread it, I find another unobtrusive flicker of connection between the sixteenth-century tale and the modern one. My moment of inordinate private laughter was over the table in the ultramodern Villa Hodgkiss, a truly Italian overdesigned misfit.

> In the centre was placed, in fact fixed, a round table of pale green marble, with the shapes of twelve plates, twelve knives, twelve forks, let into the surface in darker green mosaic. On an evening such as this when only eight guests were dining, none of the real plates, knives or forks quite covered their green stone images. The Institute, presumably, had not liked to argue on this point with their architect, who had reserved the right to design all the furniture, much of it immovable. And there was no place at all indicated for the spoons, which looked like intruders.

This is shrewd cultural observation. It is also a quiet, harmless example of an unyieldingness like that of the midget Ridolfi in 1568.

Human Voices (with its echo of *Prufrock*) and *Innocence* are perfect titles for their books. So is *The Beginning of Spring* (1988), which is set in Moscow in 1913, before both the Russian Revolution and the First World War. Its hero is

Frank Reid, owner and manager of Reid's, a British print-
ing firm set up in the 1870s. At the beginning of the novel
Frank's wife, Nellie, has suddenly left with his three children, subsequently abandoning them at a railway station.
They are, like all Fitzgerald's child characters, intelligent
and resourceful, aware of the deficiencies of their elders.
Frank is also resourceful, and the novel is an account of his
attempts to construct a life, engage a young woman (possibly a revolutionary) to look after them, and avoid the kind-
nesses of the expatriate community and his emotional Russian acquaintances and business connections. The novel is
as Russian as *Innocence* is Italian; the muddles are Russian
muddles, the suspicions and warmth and vaguenesses are
Russian. The weather, winter and spring, the river and its
ice floes, the dacha and the birch forest, are Russian. As
with *Innocence,* what look like comic set pieces of misunderstanding turn out to be integral parts of the mystery and
the plot. For a writer who selects every phrase as carefully
and with as clear an ear as a poet, Fitzgerald has a re-
markably intricate and satisfying way with plot and narra-
tive too. There are beginnings, middles, and ends, and they
are not disappointing; indeed, they are both shocking and
satisfactory. There are wonderful scenes in a teahouse
with a traveling samovar, in a Dostoyevskian nursery with
a bewildered new pet bear cub. The English are suspi-
cious, narrow, provincial, and substantial. Again there is a
dangerous innocent, Selwyn Crane, an English devotee of

Tolstoy's asceticism, an absurd vegetarian, author of the poems *Birch Tree Thoughts,* which provide both an unexpected part of the intrigue and a moment of pure laughter. Only a writer with a very good ear could have produced the exemplary dotty lameness of

> "Dost feel the cold, sister birch?"
> "No, Brother Snow,
> I feel it not." "What? not?" "No, not!"

In *The Beginning of Spring* the private story and the private world are at the center; we know that Fitzgerald, by whatever mysterious means, knows abundantly more about the world her people move in than she tells us, although it is a lost and distant one. She has done so much reading, so much research, that she can select the telling detail, the particular smell, sound, or object, as she could from the world she lives in daily. It is *underresearched* novels that smell of the lamp and in the end don't ring true. And for that reason, Fitzgerald's grasp on the larger world is assured too. The revolution is coming, with the spring, in this book. But the people are plunged in the purposeful private and commercial muddle of their single, not exemplary lives.

The Gate of Angels (1990) is also set in that unknowing time (1912, precisely) just before the First World War. It concerns the life of Fred Fairly, a Cambridge physicist, son of a country vicar, who has lost his religious faith. He means to work with his hero, Rutherford, on atomic research, but ends up working with a Professor Flowerdew, who is skeptical about working with "unobservables," saying that this will lead to randomness, laws acting in "a profoundly disorderly way," wild ideas such as "anti-matter which is supposed to be there but isn't," and ultimately "chaos." Fred is a member of a college with no students, into which no woman may ever penetrate, not even as a servant, and he is made by a friend to speak at a club called the Disobligers' Society in favor of the existence of the soul, in which he does not believe. He makes a good case, in a wild way, for the separate existence of mind. Someone remarks that "Fairly perhaps, sees a bird flying over the fens, and he looks attentively at a young woman, and he combines the two of them, and imagines an angel. That is how the imagination works. However, no two people see the external world in exactly the same way. To every separate person a thing is what he thinks it is—in other words, not a thing, but a think."

This is, among other things, a statement of a Romantic philosophical position—the mind creates and constructs the world it lives in. Both angels and atomic particles are "unobservables" which need minds in order to come out of chaos. As we know, physicists now think observing minds affect the behavior of particles. Fitzgerald's next novel, *The Blue Flower*, concerns German Romanticism. Her novel about science in the Cambridge of 1912 is a religious novel

about the life and well-being of the individual soul in a
world of material probabilities. The great nineteenth-century novels were excited by positive science, by the representative life, the detail that showed the shape of historic
and material circumstances. I have said that Fitzgerald's
earlier novels had a surreal quality to their comedy. Like
the surrealists, Fitzgerald asserts the reality of the individual, the improbable, the singleton. Her invisible world is
peopled by angels, poltergeists (see *The Bookshop*), and
random particles. Fred falls in love with Daisy, an angel
in the common metaphoric sense, as she is a nurse (and
a good one). He meets her by a most improbable coincidence, or material collision, when they are separately
struck by an out-of-control farm cart while riding bicycles
across the fen. They wake to find themselves naked, side by
side, in the attic of a strange Cambridge couple. Daisy, although unmarried, is wearing a wedding ring (for reasons
circuitously revealed), so they are thought to be husband
and wife. The Cambridge of fusty bachelors, principled
eccentrics, early suffragists, and ghost stories à la M. R.
James is as meticulously put together, piece by glittering
piece, as Florence or Moscow. The ghost story is itself a
materialist form which asserts the existence of spirit where
it shouldn't be or isn't expected to be. Outrageous coincidence and improbability are used as formal devices to
suggest that the world of the typical and the probable may
not be all. The finale is brilliant: a woman (Daisy) walks

through the never-opened Gate of Angels in the college, saves the life of a man who cannot see her (the blind master of the college), and is thereby delayed sufficiently to collide again with the rejected Frank and convert a miserable series of misunderstandings into a happy ending. It is a Hardyesque coincidence, used knowingly to empower fiction and the imagination.

The Blue Flower (1995) is an improbable masterpiece. The title comes from a fairy tale in *Heinrich von Ofterdingen* where a man is obsessed with the desire to find a mysterious blue flower. The tale is by Fritz (or Friedrich) von Hardenberg, known as Novalis, a pupil of Fichte, who died at the age of twenty-eight. He became a Romantic myth and had complicated and interesting ideas about the nature of language (and philosophy and mathematics) as a system of signs, and about the relations of body and spirit. His father found him employment as a salt inspector, and he thought about the life and language of minerals. Fitzgerald's novel recreates, in brief, fleeting, evocatively real scenes, the life of two or three interconnecting families in eighteenth-century Germany, in Jena and rural Saxony. The Hardenbergs were a large, idiosyncratic family in straitened circumstances. Fitzgerald has created the touch, smell, cold, damp, slowness, and tension of a household, its meals, its habits of communication, its laundry, its disputes and intense affections, often in one or two sentences.

The story of Hardenberg's life is simple and startling.

He fell in love, at first sight, with a twelve-year-old girl, Sophie von Kühn, to whom he became engaged. She died of tuberculosis at the age of fifteen. Hardenberg created a Romantic myth around her memory, turning her into a figure of Wisdom, a Sancta Sophia. He, and his brothers and sisters, died in their twenties of pulmonary tuberculosis.

The world of *The Blue Flower* is created out of the solid, detailed life of the letters and diaries of his family (and Sophie) and is shot through with the vision and intelligence of Hardenberg's work. Early in the novel Fitzgerald quotes a letter from Friedrich Schlegel in which he describes "a young man, from whom everything may be expected, and he explained himself to me at once with fire — with indescribably much fire . . . On the first evening he told me that the golden age would return, and that there was nothing evil in the world. I don't know if he is still of the same opinion." (It is like Fitzgerald to end her quotation quietly on that dubious note.) As a boy Fritz was expelled from the Moravian school where he was sent because he would not answer correctly in the children's catechism. "A child of not quite ten years old, he insists that the body is not flesh, but the same stuff as the soul." He goes to live with the stolid Just family while working in the salt mines, and is rebuked on his arrival for telling their niece, Karoline, that she is beautiful. Frau Just says

> "You ought not to speak to Karoline quite like that. You did not mean it, and she is not used to it."

"But I did mean it," said Fritz. "When I came into your house everything, the wine-decanter, the tea, the sugar, the chairs, the dark green tablecloth with its abundant fringe, everything was illuminated."

He brings this genuine illumination into people's lives, especially Karoline's, but he is another of Fitzgerald's innocents, and scatters hurt with his failure to notice feelings or problems. There are bitter and beautiful scenes when he tells Karoline he has fallen in love with Sophie after a quarter of an hour (and that Karoline knows nothing about desire), and when he brusquely refuses the one gift his mother is able to offer him. Karoline sees Sophie clearly: an ordinary preadolescent, a hearty girl who laughs too loudly and too much. She herself, like all the women in the novel, is caught in a material world *not* transfigured by romantic light. She listens to Fritz's poems fresh from "the work of the forewinter — sausage-making, beating flax for the winter spinning, killing the geese (who had already been plucked alive twice) for their third and last crop of down. After this it was necessary to eat baked goose for a week." There is a gulf between the geese and Fritz's transfigured tablecloth, but it is a gulf that is bridged by Fitzgerald's own art, making the geese in their turn unforgettable. The reader, caught up in Karoline's never-described emotions, is ready to dislike Sophie for her brashness, nullity, and mindless laughter. But she becomes in turn the object of Fitzgerald's intelligent and unwavering imagination of disaster. There is a terrible moment when, already very ill, she visits the Hardenbergs for her engagement party wearing a white cap. Fritz's brother asks her for a lock of her hair. "Sophie laughed. She had been laughing, it was true, most of the evening, but not with such enjoyment as she did now."

It is her cousin, Frau Mandelsloh, another of Fitzgerald's practical women, who tells him that Sophie has lost all her hair, as the illness progressed, and is quite bald. Fitzgerald also describes the terrible and pointless surgical operations (without anesthetic) that Sophie undergoes. The net effect of this is to make the very ordinary Sophie the tragic center of the novel. (Hardenberg kept away from her deathbed.) It might be possible to say that Fitzgerald invests the mundane Sophie, with her laugh and her interest in smoked eel and cabbage, with the light that is absent from Hardenberg's idealized "Philosophy." But that, too, is to simplify. Toward the very end of this short novel (most of its chapters are a mere two or three pages) Fitzgerald quotes Novalis's "Algebra, like laudanum, deadens pain" in a meditation where he writes of his experiences of the certainty of immortality, of the radiance of the Justs' house, of his sense that

> we are the enemies of the world and foreigners to this earth. Our grasp of it is a process of estrangement. Through estrangement itself I earn my living from day to day. I say, this is animate but that is inanimate. I am a Salt Inspector, this is rock salt. I go further than this, much fur-

ther, and say this is waking, this is a dream, this belongs to
the body, that to the spirit, this belongs to space and distance, that to time and duration. But space spills over into
time, as the body into the soul, so that one cannot be mea-
sured without the other.

Fitzgerald sees Hardenberg's moral shortcomings clearly,
but she also sees his vision. And he too is young, unique,
and shortly to die. Part of the extraordinary composed and
moving effect of this novel is its sense of the finite, the finished nature of these long-dead people we see living and
feeling and hoping. At the very beginning Fritz rescues his
youngest brother, Bernhard, from drowning; at the end
Fitzgerald tells us Bernhard was drowned in the Saale on
November 28, 1800.

Hardenberg's musings on the nature of rock salt, time,
and space take us back to Fred Fairly, the physicist, brood-
ing on the nature of random particles. In Ian Hacking's
brilliant account of the development of our ideas of statis-
tical probability and chance, *The Taming of Chance,* he
writes of Prussian collecting of mining statistics in what
Goethe called "our statistically minded times." Statistics
and the idea of probability led to the great nineteenth-
century novels, such as Zola's, where human beings lived
out exemplary fates, moved by social forces. In a later chapter, Hacking writes of the Romantic desire to recreate the
idea of *pure chance*, about which he quotes Nietzsche's
Zarathustra, blessing "the heaven accident, the heaven

innocence, the heaven chance, the heaven prankishness."

Hacking introduces Nietzsche's homage to randomness (which is a form of necessity) by quoting Novalis, who, he said, had written in 1797 that chance manifests the miraculous. The individual "is individualised by one single chance event alone, that is, his birth." It is this understanding, what might be called a religious understanding of the individual, that gives shape to Penelope Fitzgerald's novels. Chance makes farce and chance makes disaster; in between these we construct our own identities as best we may. The Hardenbergs, and Sophie, are statistics of the devastating power of tuberculosis. Fitzgerald's art insists that they are also all individuals, body and soul.

Fitzgerald's short stories seem to me to fall into two (possibly more) groups. The first is the English well-made tale, the kind written by Elizabeth Taylor, on the one hand, and the great master of the supernatural, M. R. James, on the other. It could be argued that the well-made tales — all the stories in this collection except "The Means of Escape" and "At Hiruharama" — are about truth and illusion, and turn on the difficulty and necessity of true judgment. Fitzgerald's first novel — her earliest fiction, I believe — was *The Golden Child*, which works within the conventions of the detective story. In the same way, "The Axe" is an M. R. James ghost story, and "Not Shown" works out from the kind of tale told by Evelyn Waugh and Muriel Spark about

British social conventions, with an underlying religious judgment. Consider the authorial interpolation in the description of the grotesque Mrs. Horrabin in "Not Shown": "She belonged to the tribe of torturers. Why pretend they don't exist?" "The Prescription" is a story in which a moral riddle becomes a central mystery. It ends with the question "Knowledge is good, but what is the use of knowledge without honesty?" which shifts the moral balance between the two doctors, Mehmet Bey and his almost murdered ex-apprentice, Zarifi. This is a deliberately puzzling tale that does not allow easy sympathy for anyone and yet insists on moral examination. It is a parable whose meaning is not clear. "The Red-Haired Girl" is also well made morally. It is easy to miss the connection between the disappearance of the model, Anny, and the painter who has chosen her, and in its way it is a tour de force. "Desideratus" also is a kind of parable. It is about a medal bearing the one word *Desideratus,* which its owner, Jack Digby, believes means "long-wished for," though he is told it is not an exact translation. It is a shining keepsake. "But anything you carry about with you in your pocket you are bound to lose sooner or later," the Fitzgerald voice, entirely practical and entirely mysterious, tells us. What is lost is found, under inches of immovable ice, and lost again, and found again, in a strange and sinister household. Jack is offered a sum of money for the keepsake, but (possibly because the sum is not specified, the narrator tells us) chooses the keepsake. This tale, though there are echoes of M. R. James and maybe MacDonald, is more purely Fitzgerald's own. It has some of the atmosphere of *The Gate of Angels,* in which everything has a sufficient material existence and yet is shot through with a spiritual and possibly moral significance, hard to decipher or to discern. Who is the red-headed boy in the house, who resembles Chatterton? What is the meaning of the talismanic medallion? In Fitzgerald's world things have meaning by nature, but the meanings are problematic.

In *The Gate of Angels,* there is a ghost story with a meaning. Dr. Matthews, the provost of (the imaginary) James's, is baffled by the evidence about the accident involving Fred Fairly and his bicycle, and the fact that "the carter who was responsible for the accident has disappeared." Dr. Matthews, the Fitzgerald narrator tells us with her usual precision, "had come to regard it as much more mysterious than it really was." He is an M. R. James addict and writes an M. R. James ghost story to "explain" the mystery, employing terrifying decrepit nuns, living burial under a fenny road, and a human body pulled and distorted into a kind of sausage. It is gruesome and formally complete. It contradicts the idea most writers have that a story, a tale, is in some deep imaginative sense "truer" than fact. It operates like gossip, spreading the idea that murder and burial are involved in the "accident" (which was an accident) and precipitating the trial that nearly separates Fred and Daisy (but also helps to unite them). It is a harmless fiction that is not harmless. It is also part of the imaginative world of the novel, which also contains the habits of mind of physicists, Darwinians, statisticians, nurses, and angels.

I have written all this because I want to end by saying that, as I have argued about Fitzgerald's late novels, the two longer stories, set in the Southern Hemisphere, are concerned primarily with chance as destiny, with the revelation of spiritual form in a world of haphazard facts. "The Means of Escape" and "At Hiruharama" grew out of historical facts that Fitzgerald met while traveling and was struck by. They depend—like the tragedy of *The Blue Flower*, like the comedy of *The Gate of Angels*, like *Innocence* and *The Beginning of Spring*—on the writer's recognizing chance patterns, the forms of coincidence and improbability and accident, and using them to suggest an underlying spiritual destiny, or anyway a significance, that is undeniable. I don't want to reveal the two stories' surprises, for they are their essence; they are the apparently unimportant facts—carrier pigeons and convict hoods, prison garb and afterbirths—out of which a glittering structure is made. The horror of the plot of "The Axe" is implicit in its conventional shape. But these two tales could go anywhere, and where they *do* go gives a greater aesthetic satisfaction—and sheer pleasure of reading—than any conventional fulfillment.

I included "At Hiruharama" in *The Oxford Book of English Short Stories,* a collection confined to the English

English, not simply to the English language. I found that the English stories I liked best were inconsequential; they broke rules, were surreally real. The best metaphor I could find for the precise quality I was trying to locate was in *The Knox Brothers,* in one of Penelope's descriptions of an uncle of hers at an English public school. It is a very short story in itself.

> One midday a boy threw a squash ball which exactly struck the hands of the great clock that set the time for the whole school and stopped it. Masters and boys, drawing their watches out of their pockets as they hurried across the yard, to compare the false with the true, were thrown into utter confusion. It turned out that the boy, who confessed at once, had been practising the shot for two years. The Bodger [a schoolmaster] called this "un-English." Eddie did not agree. The patient, self-contained, self-imposed pursuit of an entirely personal solution seemed to him most characteristically English.

This — the exact physical act, with its metaphysical overtone of false and true time, of stopping intolerable authoritative time — seems to me pure Fitzgerald. Another clever, resourceful, eccentric child produces a patient, self-contained, idiosyncratic solution. Her stories, of both kinds, are such solutions. I only wish she had found time to write more.

A. S. Byatt

The Means of Escape

ST. GEORGE'S CHURCH, Hobart, stands high above Battery Point and the harbor. Inside, it looks strange and must always have done so, although (at the time I'm speaking of) it didn't have the blue-, pink- and yellow-patterned stained glass that you see there now. That was ordered from a German firm in 1875. But St. George's has always had the sarcophagus-shaped windows, which the architect had thought Egyptian and therefore appropriate (St. George is said to have been an Egyptian saint). They give you the curious impression, as you cross the threshold, of entering a tomb.

In 1852, before the organ was installed, the church used to face east, and music was provided by a seraphine. The seraphine was built, and indeed invented, by a Mr. Ellard, formerly of Dublin, now a resident of Hobart. He intended it to suggest the angelic choir, although the singing voices at his disposal—the surveyor general, the naval chaplain, the harbormaster and their staffs—were for the most part male. Who was able to play the seraphine? Only, at first, Mr. Ellard's daughter, Mrs. Logan, who seems to have got £20 a year for doing so, the same fee as the clerk and the sexton. When Mrs. Logan began to feel the task was too much for her—the seraphine needs continuous pumping —she instructed Alice Godley, the rector's daughter.

Hobart stands "south of no north," between snowy Mount Wellington and the River Derwent, running down over steps and promontories to the harbor's bitterly cold water. You get all the winds that blow. The next stop to the south is the limit of the Antarctic drift ice. When Alice went up to practice the hymns she had to unlock the outer storm door, made of Huon pine, and the inner door, also a storm door, and drag them shut again.

The seraphine stood on its own square of Axminster carpet in the transept. Outside (at the time I'm speaking of) it was a bright afternoon, but inside St. George's there was that mixture of light and inky darkness which suggests that from the darkness something may be about to move. It was difficult, for instance, to distinguish whether among the black-painted pews, at some distance away, there was or wasn't some person or object rising above the level of the seats. Alice liked to read mystery stories, when she could get hold of them, and the thought struck her now: The form of a man is advancing from the shadows.

If it had been ten years ago, when she was still a school-girl, she might have shrieked out, because at that time there were said to be bolters and escaped convicts from Port Arthur on the loose everywhere. The constabulary hadn't been put on to them. Now there were only a few names of runaways, perhaps twenty, posted on the notice boards outside Government House.

"I did not know that anyone was in the church," she said. "It is kept locked. I am the organist. Perhaps I can assist you?"

A rancid stench, not likely from someone who wanted to be shown round the church, came towards her up the aisle. The shape, too, seemed wrong. But that, she saw, was because the head was hidden in some kind of sack like a butchered animal, or, since it had eye holes, more like a man about to be hanged.

"Yes," he said, "you can be of assistance to me."

"I think now that I can't be," she said, picking up her music case. "No nearer," she added distinctly.

He stood still, but said, "We shall have to get to know one another better." And then, "I am an educated man. You may try me out if you like, in Latin and some Greek. I have come from Port Arthur. I was a poisoner."

"I should not have thought you were old enough to be married."

"I never said I poisoned my wife!" he cried.

"Were you innocent, then?"

"You women think that everyone in jail is innocent. No, I'm not innocent, but I was wrongly incriminated. I never lifted a hand. They criminated me on false witness."

"I don't know about lifting a hand," she said. "You mentioned that you were a poisoner."

"My aim in saying that was to frighten you," he said. "But that is no longer my aim at the moment."

It had been her intention to walk straight out of the church, managing the doors as quickly as she could, and on no account looking back at him, since she believed that with a man of bad character, as with a horse, the best thing was to show no emotion whatever. He, however, moved round through the pews in such a manner as to block her way.

He told her that the name he went by, which was not his given name, was Savage. He had escaped from the Model Penitentiary. He had a knife with him, and had thought at first to cut her throat, but had seen almost at once that the young lady was not on the cross. He had got into the church tower (which was half finished, but no assigned labor could be found to work on it at the moment) through the gaps left in the brickwork. Before he could ask for food, she told him firmly that she herself could get him none. Her father was the incumbent, and the most generous of men, but at the Rectory they had to keep very careful count of everything, because charity was given out at the door every Tuesday and Thursday evening. She might be able to bring him the spent tea leaves, which were always kept, and he could mash them again if he could find warm water.

"That's a sweet touch!" he said. "Spent tea leaves!"

"It is all I can do now, but I have a friend—I may perhaps be able to do more later. However, you can't stay here beyond tomorrow."

"I don't know what day it is now."

"It is Wednesday, the twelfth of November."

"Then *Constancy* is still in harbor."

"How do you know that?"

It was all they did know for certain in the penitentiary. There was a rule of absolute silence, but the sailing lists were passed secretly among those who could read, and memorized from them by those who could not.

"*Constancy* is a converted collier, carrying cargo and a hundred and fifty passengers, laying at Franklin Wharf. I am entrusting you with my secret intention, which is to stow on her to Portsmouth, or as far at least as Cape Town."

He was wearing grey felon's slops. At this point he took off his hood and stood wringing it round and round in his hands, as though he were trying to wash it.

Alice looked at him directly for the first time.

"I shall need a change of clothing, ma'am."

"You may call me Miss Alice," she said.

At the prompting of some sound, or imaginary sound, he retreated and vanished up the dark gap, partly boarded up, of the staircase to the tower. That which had been on

his head was left in a heap on the pew. Alice took it up and
put it into her music case, pulling the strap tight.

She was lucky in having a friend very much to her own
mind, Aggie, the daughter of the people who ran Shuckburgh's Hotel; Aggie Shuckburgh, in fact.

"He might have cut your throat, did you think of that?"

"He thought better of it," said Alice.

"What I should like to know is this: why didn't you
go straight to your father, or to Colonel Johnson at the
Constabulary? I don't wish you to answer me at once, because it mightn't be the truth. But tell me this: Would you
have acted in the same manner if it had been a woman
hiding in the church?" Alice was silent, and Aggie asked,
"Did a sudden strong warmth spring up between the two
of you?"

"I think that it did."

No help for it, then, Aggie thought. "He'll be hard put to
it, I'm afraid. There's no water in the tower, unless the last
lot of builders left a pailful, and there's certainly no dunny."

But Alice thought he might slip out by night. "That is
what I should do myself, in his place." She explained that
Savage was an intelligent man, and that he intended to stow
away on *Constancy*.

"My dear, you're not thinking of following him."

"I'm not thinking at all," said Alice.

They were in the hotel, checking the clean linen. So
many tablecloths; so many aprons, kitchen; so many

aprons, dining room; so many pillow shams. They hardly ever talked without working. They knew their duties to both their families

Shuckburgh's had its own warehouse and bond store on the harborfront. Aggie would find an opportunity to draw out, not any of the imported goods, but at least a ration of tea and bacon. Then they could see about getting it up to the church.

"As long as you didn't imagine it, Alice!"

Alice took her arm. "Forty-five!"

They had settled on the age of forty-five to go irredeemably cranky. They might start imagining anything they liked then. The whole parish, indeed the whole neighborhood, thought that they were cranky already, in any case, not to get settled, Aggie in particular, with all the opportunities that came her way in the hotel trade.

"He left this behind," said Alice, opening her music case, which let fly a feral odor. She pulled out the sacking mask, with its slits, like a mourning Pierrot's, for eyes.

"Do they make them wear those?"

"I've heard Father speak about them often. They wear them every time they go out of their cells. They're part of the new system; they have to prove their worth. With the masks on, none of the other prisoners can tell who a man is, and he can't tell who they are. He mustn't speak either, and that drives a man into himself, so that he's alone with the Lord, and can't help but think over his wrongdoing and repent. I never saw one of them before today, though."

"It's got a number on it," said Aggie, not going so far as to touch it. "I daresay they put them to do their own laundry."

At the Rectory there were five people sitting down already to the four o'clock dinner. Next to her father was a guest, the visiting preacher; next to him was Mrs. Watson, the housekeeper. She had come to Van Diemen's Land with a seven-year sentence, and now had her ticket of leave. Assigned servants usually ate in the back house, but in the rector's household all were part of the same family. Then, the Lukes. They were penniless immigrants (his papers had Mr. Luke down as a scene painter, but there was no theatre in Hobart). He had been staying, with his wife, for a considerable time.

Alice asked them all to excuse her for a moment while she went up to her room. Once there, she lit a piece of candle and burned the lice off the seams of the mask. She put it over her head. It did not disarrange her hair, the neat smooth hair of a minister's daughter, always presentable on any occasion. But the eye holes came too low down, so that she could see nothing and stood there in stifling darkness. She asked herself, "Wherein have I sinned?"

Her father, who never raised his voice, called from downstairs, "My dear, we are waiting." She took off the mask, folded it, and put it in the hamper where she kept her woollen stockings.

After grace they ate red snapper, boiled mutton and

bread pudding, no vegetables. In England the Reverend Alfred Godley had kept a good kitchen garden, but so far he had not been able to get either leeks or cabbages going in the thin earth round Battery Point.

Mr. Luke hoped that Miss Alice had found her time at the instrument well spent.

"I could not get much done," she answered. "I was interrupted."

"Ah, it's a sad thing for a performer to be interrupted. The concentration of the mind is gone. 'When the lamp is shattered . . .'"

"That is not what I felt at all," said Alice.

"You are too modest to admit it."

"I have been thinking, Father," said Alice, "that since Mr. Luke cares so much for music, it would be a good thing for him to try the seraphine himself. Then if by any chance I had to go away, you would be sure of a replacement."

"You speak as if my wife and I should be here always," cried Mr. Luke.

Nobody made any comment on this — certainly not Mrs. Luke, who passed her days in a kind of incredulous stupor. How could it be that she was sitting here eating bread pudding some twelve thousand miles from Clerkenwell, where she had spent all the rest of her life? The rector's attention had been drawn away by the visiting preacher, who had taken out a copy of the *Hobart Town Daily Courier* and was reading aloud a paragraph which announced his arrival from Melbourne.

"Bringing your welcome with you," the rector exclaimed. "I am glad the *Courier* noted it."

"Oh, they would not have done," said the preacher, "but I make it my practice to call in at the principal newspaper offices wherever I go, and make myself known with a few friendly words. In that way, if the editor has nothing of great moment to fill up his sheet, which is frequently the case, it is more than likely that he will include something about my witness." He had come on a not very successful mission to pray that gold would never be discovered in Van Diemen's Land, as it had been on the mainland, bringing with it the occasion of new temptations.

After the dishes were cleared Alice said she was going back for a while to Aggie's, but would, of course, be home before dark. Mr. Luke, while his wife sat on with half-closed eyes, came out to the back kitchen and asked Mrs. Watson, who was at the sink, whether he could make himself useful by pumping up some more water.

"No," said Mrs. Watson.

Mr. Luke persevered. "I believed you to have had considerable experience of life. Now, I find Miss Alice charming, but somewhat difficult to understand. Will you tell me something about her?"

"No."

Mrs. Watson was, at the best of times, a very silent woman, whose life had been an unfortunate one. She had lost three children before being transported, and could not now remember what they had been called. Alice, however, did not altogether believe this, as she had met other women who thought it unlucky to name their dead children. Mrs. Watson had surely been out of luck with her third, a baby, who had been left in the charge of a little girl of ten, a neighbor's daughter, who acted as nursemaid for four-pence a week. How the house came to catch fire was not known. It was a flash fire. Mrs. Watson was out at work. The man she lived with was in the house, but he was very drunk, and doing—she supposed—the best he could under the circumstances, he pitched both the neighbor's girl and the baby out of the window. The coroner had said that it might just as well have been a Punch and Judy show. "Try to think no more about it," Alice advised her. As chance would have it, Mrs. Watson had been taken up only a week later for thieving. She had tried to throw herself in the river, but the traps had pulled her out again.

On arrival in Hobart, she had been sent to the Female Factory, and later, after a year's steady conduct, to the Hiring Depot where employers could select a pass holder. That was how, several years ago, she had fetched up at the Rectory. Alice had taught her to write and read, and had given her (as employers were required to do in any case) a copy of the Bible. She handed over the book with a kiss. On the flyleaf she had copied out a verse from Hosea: "Say to your sister, Ruhamah, you have obtained mercy."

Mrs. Watson had no documents which indicated her age, and her pale face was not so much seamed or lined as knocked, apparently, out of the true by a random blow which might have been time or chance. Perhaps she had always looked like that. Although she said nothing by way of thanks at the time, it was evident, as the months went by, that she had transferred the weight of unexpended affection, which is one of a woman's greatest inconveniences, on to Miss Alice. This was clear partly from the way she occasionally caught hold of Alice's hand and held it for a while, and from her imitation, sometimes unconsciously grotesque, of Alice's rapid walk and her way of doing things about the house.

Aggie had the tea, the bacon, the plum jam, and, on her own initiative, had added a roll of tobacco. This was the only item from the bond store and perhaps should have been left alone, but neither of the girls had ever met or heard of a man who didn't smoke or chew tobacco if he had the opportunity. They knew that on Norfolk Island and at Port Arthur the convicts sometimes killed for tobacco.

They had a note of the exact cash value of what was taken. Alice would repay the amount to Shuckburgh's Hotel from the money she earned from giving music lessons. (She had always refused to take a fee for playing the seraphine at St. George's.) But what of truth's claim, what of honesty's? Well, Alice would leave, say, a hundred and twenty days for *Constancy* to reach Portsmouth. Then she would go to her father.

"What will you say to him?" Aggie asked.

"I shall tell him that I have stolen and lied, and caused my friend to steal and lie."

"Yes, but that was all in the name of the corporeal mercies. You felt pity for this man, who had been a prisoner and was alone in the wide world."

"I am not sure that what I feel is pity."

Certainly the two of them must have been seen through the shining front windows of the new terraced houses on their way up to the church. Certainly they were seen with their handcart, but this was associated with parish magazines and requests for a subscription to something or other, so that at the sight of it the watchers left their windows. At the top of the rise Aggie, who was longing to have a look at Alice's lag, said, "I'll not come in with you."

"But Aggie, you've done so much, and you'll want to see his face."

"I do want to see his face, but I'm keeping myself in check. That's what forms the character, keeping yourself in check at times."

"Your character is formed already, Aggie."

"Sakes, Alice, do you want me to come in with you?"

"No."

*

"Mr. Savage," she called out decisively.

"I am just behind you."

Without turning round, Alice counted out the packages in their stout wrappings of whitish paper. He did not take them, not even the tobacco, but said, "I have been watching you and the other young lady from the tower."

"This situation can't continue," said Alice. "There is the regular Moonah Men's prayer meeting on Friday."

"I shall make a run for it tomorrow night," said Savage, "but I need women's clothing. I am not of heavy build. The flesh came off me at Port Arthur, one way and another. Can you furnish me?"

"I must not bring women's clothes to the church," said Alice. "St. Paul forbids it." But she had often felt that she was losing patience with St. Paul.

"If he won't let you come to me, I must come to you," said Savage.

"You mean to my father's house?"

"Tell me the way exactly, Miss Alice, and which your room is. As soon as the time's right, I will knock twice on your window."

"You will not knock on it once!" said Alice. "I don't sleep on the ground floor."

"Does your room face the sea?"

"No, I don't care to look at the sea. My window looks onto the Derwent, up the river valley to the northwest."

Now that she was looking at him, he put his two thumbs

and forefingers together in a sign which she had understood and indeed used herself ever since she was a child. It meant *I give you my whole heart.*

"I should have thought you might have wanted to know what I was going to do when I reached England," he said.

"I do know. You'll be found out, taken up and committed to Pentonville as an escaped felon."

"Only give me time, Miss Alice, and I will send for you."

In defiance of any misfortune that might come to him, he would send her the needful money for her fare and his address, once he had a home for her, in England.

"Wait and trust, give me time, and I will send for you."

In low-built, shipshape Battery Point the Rectory was unusual in being three stories high, but it had been smartly designed with ironwork Trafalgar balconies, and the garden had been planted with English roses as well as daisy bushes and silver wattle. It was the rector's kindheartedness which had made it take on the appearance of a human warren. Alice's small room, as she had told Savage, looked out on the river. Next to her, on that side of the house, was the visiting preacher's room, always called, as in the story of Elijah, the prophet's chamber. The Lukes faced the sea, and the rector had retreated to what had once been his study. Mrs. Watson slept at the back, over the wash house, which projected from the kitchen. Above were the box rooms, all inhabited by a changing population of no-hopers, thrown out of work by the depression of the 1840s. These people did not eat at the Rectory — they went to the Colonial Families' Charitable on Knopwood Street — but their washing and their poultry had given the grass plot the air of a seedy encampment, ready to surrender at the first emergency.

Alice did not undress the following night, but lay down in her white blouse and waist. One of her four shawls and one of her three skirts lay folded over the back of the sewing chair. At first she lay there and smiled, then almost laughed out loud at the notion of Savage, like a mummer in a Christmas pantomime, struggling down the Battery steps and onto the wharves under the starlight in her nankeen petticoat. Then she ceased smiling, partly because she felt the unkindness of it, partly because of her perplexity as to why he needed to make this very last part of his run in skirts. Did he have in mind to set sail as a woman?

She let her thoughts run free. She knew perfectly well that Savage, after years of enforced solitude, during which he had been afforded no prospect of a woman's love, was unlikely to be coming to her room just for a bundle of clothes. If he wanted to get into bed with her, what then? Ought she to raise the house? She imagined calling out (though not until he was gone), and her door opening, and the bare shanks of the rescuers jostling in in their night-shirts — the visiting preacher, Mr. Luke, her father, the up-stairs lodgers — and she prayed for grace. She thought of the forgiven: Rahab the harlot of Jericho, the wife of Hosea who had been a prostitute, Mary Magdalene, Mrs. Watson who had cohabited with a drunken man.

You may call me Miss Alice.

I will send for you.

You could not hear St. George's clock from the Rectory. She marked the hours from the clock at Government House on the waterfront. It had been built by convict labor and intended first of all as the Customs House. It was now three o'clock. The *Constancy* sailed at first light.

Give me time and I will send for you.

If he had been seen leaving the church, and arrested, they would surely have come to tell the rector. If he had missed the way to the Rectory and been caught wandering in the streets, then no one else was to blame but herself. I should have brought him straight home with me. He should have obtained mercy. I should have called out loud to every one of them: Look at him, this is the man who will send for me.

The first time she heard a tap at the window she lay still, thinking, He may look for me if he chooses. It was nothing, there was no one there. The second and third times, at which she got up and crossed the cold floor, were also nothing.

Alice, however, did receive a letter from Savage (he still gave himself that name). It arrived about eight months later, and had been dispatched from Portsmouth. By that time she was exceedingly busy, since Mrs. Watson had left the Rectory, and had not been replaced.

Honoured Miss Alice,

I think it only proper to do Justice to Myself, by telling you the Circumstances which took place on the 12 of November Last Year. In the First Place, I shall not forget your Kindness. Even when I go down to the Dust, as we all shall do so, a Spark will proclaim, that Miss Alice Godley Relieved me in my Distress.

Having got to the Presbittery in accordance with your Directions, I made sure first of your Room, facing North West, and got up the House the handiest way, by scaling the Wash-house Roof, intending to make the Circuit of the House by means of the Ballcony and its varse Quantity of creepers. But I was made to Pause at once by a Window opening and an Ivory Form leaning out, and a Woman's Voice suggesting a natural Proceeding between us, which there is no need to particularise. When we had done our business, she said further, You may call me Mrs. Watson, tho it is not my Name. — I said to her, I am come here in search of Woman's Clothing. I am a convict on the bolt, and it is my intention to conceal myself on Constancy, laying at Franklyn Wharf. She replied immediately, "I can Furnish you, and indeed I can see No Reason, why I should not Accompany you."

This letter of Savage's, in its complete form, is now, like so many memorials of convict days, in the National Library of Tasmania, in Hobart. There is no word in it to Alice Godley from Mrs. Watson herself. It would seem that like many people who became literate later in life, she read a great deal—the Bible in particular—but never took much to writing, and tended to mistrust it. In consequence, her motives for doing what she did—which, taking into account her intense affection for Alice, must have been complex enough—were never set down, and can only be guessed at.

The Prescription

AFTER Petros Zarifi's wife died, his shop began to make less and less money. His wife had acted as cashier. That was all over now. The shelves emptied gradually as the unpaid wholesalers refused to supply him with goods. In his tiny room at the back of the shop he had, like many Greek storekeepers, an oleograph in vivid colors of his patron saint, with the motto *Embros* — Forward! But he had now lost all ambition except in the matter of his son Alecco.

The shop was not too badly placed, on the very edge of the Phanar, where Zarifi should have been able to sell to both Greeks and Turks. One of his remaining customers, in fact, was an elderly Stamboullu who worked as dispenser to a prosperous doctor in the Beyazit district. Both old Yousuf and Dr. Mehmet drank raki, which they regarded as permissible because it had not been invented in the days of the Prophet. One evening when he was refilling the bottles Zarifi asked Yousuf to speak for him to Mehmet Bey.

"Ask him if he will take my son Alecco, who has just turned fourteen, into his employment."

"Can't his own relatives provide for him?" asked the old man.

"Don't give a father advice on this matter," said Zarifi. "What else does he think about when he lies awake at night?"

Mehmet Bey took the virtue of compassion seriously. Once he had been told that Zarifi was a good Greek, who had won a reputation for honesty, and, possibly as a result, had been unfortunate, he sent word that he would see him.

"Your son can clean my boots and run errands. That is all I have to offer. Don't let him have ambitions. There are too many doctors in Stamboul, and above all, far too many Greeks."

"Good, well, I understand you, *bey effendi,* you may trust both my son and me."

It was arranged that Alecco should work and sleep at the doctor's house in Hayreddin Pasha Street. His room was not much larger than a cupboard, but then, neither had it been at home. Loneliness was his trouble, not discomfort. The doctor's wife, Azizié Hanoum, kept to her quarters, and old Yousuf, who was a poor relation of hers, jealously guarded the dispensary, where the drugs must have been arranged in some kind of system since he was able, given time, to make up a prescription when called upon. As to Mehmet Bey himself, his hours were regular. After a sluggish evening visit to the coffee house to read the newspaper, he would return and spend a few hours more than half asleep in the bosom of his family. But Alecco understood very well, or thought he understood, what it was that his father expected him to do.

Polishing the boots of the *hakim bashi* did not take up much of the day. Always obedient, he went about with the doctor as a servant, keeping several paces behind, carrying his bag and his stethoscope. Once a week Mehmet Bey, as a good Moslem, gave his services to the hospital for the poor on the waterfront, and Alecco learned in the wards to recognize the face of leprosy and of death itself. Then, because he was so quick, he began to help a little with the accounts, and from the ledgers he gathered in a few weeks how the practice was run and which were the commonest complaints and how much could be charged for them in each case—always excepting the bills of the very rich, which were presented by Mehmet Bey in person. The doctor, for his part, recognized that this boy was sharp, and did not much like it. A subject race, he reflected, is a penance to the ruler. But he reminded himself that the father was trustworthy and honorable, and in time the son's sharpness might turn into nothing worse than industry, which is harmless.

Every day Alecco asked himself: Have I gone one step

forward or one backward? What have I learned that I didn't know yesterday? Books are teachers to those who have none, but the doctor's library reposed behind the wooden shutters of the cupboards fitted into the walls of his consulting room. His student *Materia Medica* was there, along with herbals in Arabic and the *Gulistan,* or *Rose Garden of Medicines.* Lately he had acquired a brand-new book, Gray's *Anatomy* in a French translation. Alecco had seen him turning it over heavily during the late afternoon. But it was put away with the others, and there was no chance to look at it, still less to copy the illustrations.

The dispensary also was kept locked and bolted. But that year the month of Ramadan fell in the hot weather, and both the doctor and old Yousuf, being obliged to fast all day until sunset, went out in the hours of darkness to take refreshment, Mehmet Bey at the homes of his friends, Yousuf at the teahouse. Security was less strict, and the house itself, windowless against the street, seemed to relax at the end of its tedious day. During the second week of the fast, Alecco found the door of the dispensary unfastened.

Just before dawn began to lift, Mehmet Bey returned and saw that a single candle lamp was burning in his dispensary. The Greek boy was standing at the bench, copying out prescriptions. He had also taken down a measuring glass, a pestle and a number of bottles and jars.

Bath boy, *tellak,* son of a whore, the doctor thought. The hurt pierced deep. His friends had warned him, his wife had told him he was a fool. But in the end he had made a burden for his own back.

Alecco was so deeply absorbed that his keen sense of danger failed him. He did not move until Mehmet Bey towered close behind him. Then he turned, not dropping the pen and ink which he had stolen but gripping them closely to him, and stared up with the leaden eyes of a woken sleepwalker at his master.

"I see that you are studying my prescriptions," said Mehmet Bey. "I know from experience that you learn quickly."

He picked up the empty glass. "Now, make up a medicine for yourself."

Sweating and trembling, Alecco shook in a measure of this and a measure of that, always keeping his eyes on his master. He could not have said what he was doing. Mehmet Bey, however, saw a dose of aphrodisiac go into the glass, and then the dried flowers of *Vitex agnus-castus* (which inhibits sex), opium, lavender, *Ecballium elaterium* (the most violent of all purgatives), *Datura,* either 14 grams (inducing insanity), or 22½ grams (death), and finally mustard and cinnamon. Silently he pointed to the fuller's earth, which prevents the patient from vomiting. Alecco added a handful.

"Drink!"

The doctor's voice, raised to a pitch of sacred rage, woke up Azizié Hanoum, and standing terrified in her old wrapper at the door of the women's quarters, she saw her husband seize the Greek boy by the nose, from which water poured out, and force his head backwards to dislocation point while something black as pitch ran from the measuring glass down his throat.

In the morning Alecco, who had been crammed into his room unconscious, appeared smiling with the doctor's cleaned boots in his hands. Mehmet Bey made a sign to avert evil.

"You're well? You're alive?"

"My prescription did me a world of good."

The doctor called his servants and had him turned out of the house. Picking himself up, Alecco walked away with fourteen-year-old jauntiness along the new horse tramway until he was out of sight. Not until he reached the foot of the Galata Bridge did his will power give way and he collapsed groaning like vermin on a dung hill.

Preparing slowly for his rounds, Mehmet Bey at first congratulated himself, since if the boy had died he was not quite certain how he would have stood with the law. But the household's peace was destroyed. Old Yousuf was so perturbed by the mess in the dispensary that he collapsed with a slight stroke. He had never been able to read, and now that the drugs were out of order he could find nothing. Azizié Hanoum poured reproaches on her husband and declared that if the little Greek had been better treated he could have been trained to help Yousuf. Zarifi mourned his son, who did not return either to the Phanar or to Hayreddin Pasha Street. In a few months the grocer's shop was bankrupt.

Alecco had been picked up on the waterfront by a Greek ship's cook, coming back on board after a night's absence. He had some confused idea of conciliating the captain, who, he knew, was short of a boy. The *Andromeda* was an irregular trading vessel carrying mail via Malta and Gibraltar, and by the time she reached London Alecco had been seasick to such an extent that he was clear of the poison's last traces. This seemed a kind of providence; he could never have cheated Death without some help. The captain had fancied him from the start, and when the crew were paid off at Albert Dock he gave him five pounds in English money to make a good start in life.

Ten years later Dr. Mehmet's career had reached its highest point and was also (he was sixty-five) approaching its end. Having been called, not for the first time, for consultation at the Old Serail, he settled down for a long waiting period before an attendant arrived to escort him to the anterooms. He took a seat overlooking the Sea of Marmara and resigned himself. In contemplation of the lazing water, he allowed his energies to sleep. The ladies here were the old and the pensioned off, but the appointment was an honor.

Quite without warning, and faintly disagreeable, was the appearance of a secretary: Lelia Hanoum had wished for a second opinion, and he had the honor to present a distinguished young colleague who had hurried here from another appointment. But when a young man walked in wearing a black *stambouline,* the professional's frock coat, and followed by a servant carrying his bag and stethoscope, Mehmet Bey knew not only who he was, but that he had been expecting him.

"I decline to accept you as a colleague, Alexander Zarifi."

"I am qualified," Dr. Zarifi replied.

"Your word is not good enough."

Alecco took out from the upper pocket of his *stambouline* a card printed in gilt, which showed that he had recently been appointed to attend the Serail. This could not be contradicted, and after putting it away he said:

"I am honored, then, to join you as a consultant." He waited for the usual, in fact necessary, reply: "The honor is mine." But instead Mehmet Bey said loudly: "There is no need for us to waste time in each other's company. I know the case history of Lelia Hanoum, you may consult my notes. I have already made the diagnosis. Last year the patient complained of acute pain in the left side and a distention as though a ball or globe was rising from the abdomen to the throat. Palpitations, fits of crying, quantities of wind passed per rectum. A typical case of hysteria, all too common in the Serail, and entirely the result of an ill-balanced regimen. I advised firm treatment, iron pills and a Gentian tonic. Recently, however, she has described the initial pain as on the right side. Accordingly I have changed my diagnosis to acute appendicitus, and I propose to operate as soon as permission can be got from the palace. She is rather old for the operation to be successful, but that is in God's hands."

"I cannot agree," Dr. Zarifi replied. "The very fact that the patient is uncertain whether she feels pain on the left or right side means that we must look beneath her symptoms for an unconscious or subconscious factor. During my training in Vienna I was fortunate enough to work with Dr. Josef Breuer, the great specialist in hysteria. It is for the woman herself to lead us to the hidden factor, perhaps under hypnosis. It is my belief that there is no need for medication, still less for surgical interference. We must aim at setting her free."

"Well, now I have your opinion," said Mehmet Bey. "If I reject it, it is because I have studied the art of healing, not so much from personal ambition as to answer the simplest of all appeals — *hastayim,* I am ill. I accept that since we last met you have had the advantage of a good training, but your nature will not have changed. You are still Alexander Zarifi. What is more, there are universal laws, which govern all human beings, not excepting men of science. Cast your memory back, and answer me this question: Knowledge is good, but what is the use of knowledge without honesty?"

Dr. Alecco looked down at the ground, and withdrew his diagnosis.

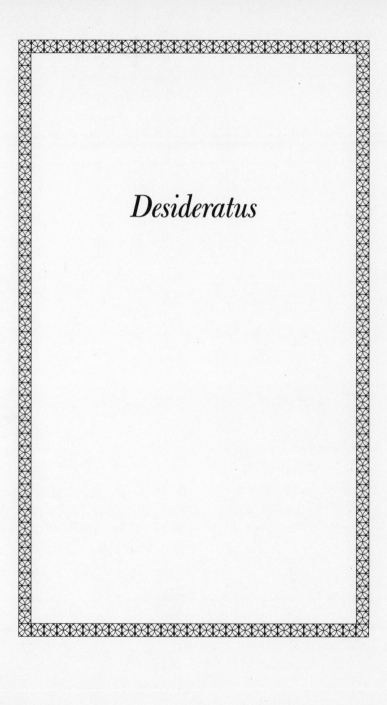

Desideratus

JACK DIGBY'S MOTHER never gave him any-thing. Perhaps, as a poor woman, she had nothing to give, or perhaps she was not sure how to divide anything among the nine children. His godmother, Mrs. Piercy, the poul-terer's wife, did give him something, a keepsake in the form of a gilt medal. The date on it was September 12, 1663, which happened to be Jack's birthday, although by the time she gave it to him he was eleven years old. On the back there was the figure of an angel and a motto, *Desideratus,* which perhaps didn't fit the case too well, since Mrs. Digby could have done with fewer, rather than more, children. However, it had taken the godmother's fancy.

Jack thanked her, and she advised him to stow it away safely, out of reach of the other children. Jack was amazed that she should think anywhere was out of the reach of his little sisters. "You should have had it earlier, when you

were born," said Mrs. Piercy, "but those were hard times."
Jack told her that he was very glad to have something of
which he could say, This is my own, and she answered,
though not with much conviction, that he mustn't set too
much importance on earthly possessions.

He kept the medal with him always, only transferring
it, as the year went by, from his summer to his winter
breeches. But anything you carry about with you in your
pocket you are bound to lose sooner or later. Jack had an
errand to do in Hending, but there was nothing on the road
that day, neither horse nor cart, no hope of cadging a lift,
so after waiting for an hour or so he began to walk over by
the hill path.

After about a mile the hill slopes away sharply towards
Watching, which is not a village and never was, only a
single great house standing among its outbuildings almost
at the bottom of the valley. Jack stopped there for a while to
look down at the smoke from the chimneys and to calcu-
late, as anyone might have done, the number of dinners
that were being cooked there that day.

If he dropped or lost his keepsake, he did not know it at
the time, for as is commonly the case he didn't miss it until
he got home again. Then he went through his pockets, but
the shining medal was gone and he could only repeat, "I
had it when I started out." His brothers and sisters were of
no help at all. They had seen nothing. What brother or
sister likes being asked such questions?

The winter frosts began and at Michaelmas Jack had the day off school and thought, I had better try going that way again. He halted, as before, at the highest point, to look down at the great house and its chimneys, and then at the ice under his feet, for all the brooks, ponds, and runnels were frozen on every side of him, all hard as bone. In a little hole or depression just to the left hand of the path, something no bigger than a small puddle, but deep, and by now set thick with greenish ice as clear as glass, he saw, through the transparency of the ice, at the depth of perhaps twelve inches, the keepsake that Mrs. Piercy had given him.

He had nothing in his hand to break the ice. Well then, Jack Digby, jump on it, but that got him nowhere, seeing that his wretched pair of boots were soaked right through. I'll wait until the ice has gone, he thought. The season is turning, we'll get a thaw in a day or two.

On the next Sunday, by which time the thaw had set in, he was up there again, and made straight for the little hole or declivity, and found nothing. It was empty, after that short time, of ice and even of water. And because the idea of recovering the keepsake had occupied his whole mind that day, the disappointment made him feel lost, like a stranger to the country. Then he noticed that there was an earthenware pipe laid straight down the side of the hill, by way of a drain, and that this must very likely have carried off the water from his hole, and everything in it. No mystery as to where it led. It joined another pipe with a wider bore, and so down, I suppose, to the stableyards, thought Jack. His Desideratus had been washed down there, he was as sure of that now as if he'd seen it go.

Jack had never been anywhere near the house before, and did not care to knock at the great kitchen doors for fear of being taken for a beggar. The yards were empty. Either the horses had been taken out to work now that the ground was softer or else — which was hard to believe — there were no horses at Watching. He went back to the kitchen wing and tried knocking at a smallish side entrance. A man came out dressed in a black gown and stood there peering and trembling.

"Why don't you take off your cap to me?" he asked.

Jack took it off and held it behind his back, as though it belonged to someone else.

"That is better. Who do you think I am?"

"No offense, sir," Jack replied, "but you look like an old schoolmaster."

"I am a schoolmaster — that is, I am tutor to this great house. If you have a question to ask, you may ask it of me."

With one foot still on the step, Jack related the story of his godmother's keepsake.

"Very good," said the tutor, "you have told me enough. Now I am going to test your memory. You will agree that this is not only necessary, but just."

"I can't see that it has anything to do with my matter," said Jack.

"Oh, but you tell me that you dropped this-or-that in such-and-such a place, and in that way lost what had been given to you. How can I tell that you have truthfully remembered all this? You know that when I came to the door you did not remember to take your cap off."

"But that—"

"You mean that was only lack of decent manners, and shows that you come from a family without self-respect. Now, let us test your memory. Do you know the Scriptures?"

Jack said that he did, and the tutor asked him what happened, in the fourth chapter of the Book of Job, to Eliphaz the Temanite when a vision came to him in the depth of the night.

"A spirit passed before his face, sir, and the hair of his flesh stood up."

"The hair of his flesh stood up," the tutor repeated. "And now, have they taught you any Latin?" Jack said that he knew the word that had been on his medal, and that it was *Desideratus,* meaning long wished-for.

"That is not an exact translation," said the tutor. Jack thought, He talks for talking's sake.

"Have you many to teach, sir, in this house?" he asked, but the tutor half closed his eyes and said, "None, none at all. God has not blessed Mr. Jonas or either of his late wives with children. Mr. Jonas has not multiplied."

If that is so, Jack thought, this schoolmaster can't have

much work to do. But now at last here was somebody with more sense, a housekeeperish woman, come to see why the side door was open and letting cold air into the passages. "What does the boy want?" she asked.

"He says he is in search of something that belongs to him."

"You might have told him to come in, then, and given him a glass of wine in the kitchen," she said, less out of kindness than to put the tutor in his place. "He would have been glad of that, I daresay."

Jack told her at once that at home they never touched wine. "That's a pity," said the housekeeper. "Children who are too strictly prohibited generally turn out drunkards." There's no pleasing these people, Jack thought.

His whole story had to be gone through again, and then again when they got among the servants in one of the pantries. Yet really there was almost nothing to tell, the only remarkable point being that he should have seen the keepsake clearly through almost a foot of ice. Still, nothing was said as to its being found in any of the yards or ponds.

Amid all the toing and froing another servant came in, the man who attended on the master, Mr. Jonas himself. His arrival caused a kind of disquiet, as though he were a foreigner. The master, he said, had got word that there was a farmboy or a schoolboy, in the kitchens, come for something that he thought was his property.

"But all this is not for Mr. Jonas's notice," cried the tutor.

"It's a story of child's stuff, a child's mischance, not at all fitting for him to look into."

The man repeated that the master wanted to see the boy.

The other part of the house, the greater part, where Mr. Jonas lived, was much quieter, the abode of gentry. In the main hall Mr. Jonas himself stood with his back to the fire. Jack had never before been alone or dreamed of being alone with such a person. What a pickle, he thought, my godmother, Mrs. Piercy, has brought me into.

"I daresay you would rather have a sum of money," said Mr. Jonas, not loudly, "than whatever it is that you have lost."

Jack was seized by a painful doubt. To be honest, if it was to be a large sum of money, he would rather have that than anything. But Mr. Jonas went on, "However, you had better understand me more precisely. Come with me." And he led the way, without even looking round to see that he was followed.

At the foot of the wide staircase Jack called out from behind, "I think, sir, I won't go any further. What I lost can't be here."

"It's poor-spirited to say 'I won't go any further,'" said Mr. Jonas.

Was it possible that on these dark upper floors no one else was living, no one was sleeping? They were like a sepulchre, or a barn at the end of winter. Through the tall passages, over uneven floors, Mr. Jonas, walking ahead, carried a candle in its candlestick in each hand, the flames pointing straight upwards. I am very far from home, thought Jack. Then, padding along behind the master of the house, and still twisting his cap in one hand, he saw in dismay that the candle flames were blown over to the left, and a door was open to the right.

"Am I to go in there with you, sir?"

"Are you afraid to go into a room?"

Inside it was dark, and in fact the room probably never got much light, the window was so high up. There was a glazed jug and basin, which reflected the candles, and a large bed which had no curtains, or perhaps, in spite of the cold, they had been drawn back. There seemed to be neither quilts nor bedding, but a boy was lying there in a linen gown, with his back towards Jack, who saw that he had red or reddish hair, much the same color as his own.

"You may go near him, and see him more clearly," Mr. Jonas said. "His arm is hanging down. What do you make of that?"

"I think it hangs oddly, sir."

He remembered what the tutor had told him, that Mr. Jonas had not multiplied his kind, and asked, "What is his name, sir?" To this he got no answer.

Mr. Jonas gestured to him to move nearer, and said, "You may take his hand."

"No, sir, I can't do that."

"Why not? You must touch other children very often.

many in a bed."

"Only three in a bed at ours," Jack muttered.

"Then touch, touch."

"No, sir, no, I can't touch the skin of him!"

Mr. Jonas set down his candles, went to the bed, took the boy's wrist and turned it so that the fingers opened. From the open fingers he took Jack's medal and gave it back to him.

"Was it warm or cold?" they asked him later. Jack told them that it was cold. Cold as ice? Perhaps not quite as cold as that.

"You have what you came for," said Mr. Jonas. "You have taken back what was yours. Note that I don't deny it was yours."

He did not move again, but stood looking down at the whitish heap on the bed. Jack was more afraid of staying than going, although he had no idea how to find his way through the house, and was lucky to come upon a back staircase which ended not where he had come in but among the sculleries, where he managed to draw back the double bolts and get out into the fresh air.

"Did the boy move," they asked him, "when the medal was taken away from him?" But by this time Jack was making up the answers as he went along. He preferred, on the whole, not to think much about Watching. It struck him, though, that he had been through a good deal to get

back his godmother's present, and he quite often wondered how much money Mr. Jonas would in fact have
offered him, if he had had the sense to accept it. Anyone who has ever been poor — even if not as poor as Jack
Digby — will sympathize with him in this matter.

Beehernz

To HOPKINS, deputy artistic director of the Midland Music Festival, an idea came. Not a new idea, but rather comforting in its familiarity, an idea for the two opening concerts next year. He put it forward, not at the preliminary meeting, still at quite an early one.

"Out of the question if it involves us in any further expense," said the chairman.

"No, it's a matter of concept," said Hopkins. "These are Mahler concerts, agreed, and we need Mahler specialists. I suggest that for the first one we book a young tearaway, no shortage of those, and for the other a retired maestro — well, they don't retire, but I have in mind a figure from the past making one of his rare appearances, venerated, dug up for the occasion, someone, perhaps, thought to be dead."

He mentioned the name of Beehernz. Most of those present had thought he was dead. Some of them remembered the name, but did not get it quite right. It was thought he had something to do with the "Symphony of a Thousand." In fact, however, he'd had nothing to do with it. Nearly forty years earlier, in 1960, the BBC had celebrated the centenary of Mahler's birth. It was only at a very late stage that Beehernz, booked for the occasion, had said, in his quiet way—that was how it had been described to Hopkins, "in his quiet way"—that he would prefer a substitute to be found for him, since he had only just learned that he was expected to conduct the Eighth Symphony.

"What is your objection to the Eighth Symphony?" he was asked.

"It is too noisy," replied Beehernz.

Beehernz had not appeared in public since that time. Hopkins's committee agreed that his name could be made into a talking point. Would Hopkins undertake the arrangements? Yes, everything, everything.

According to the BBC's records, Beehernz lived in Scotland and had done so since 1960—not on the mainland, but on an island off an island—Reilig, off Iona, off Mull, via Oban.

" 'Reilig' means 'graveyard' in Gaelic," said the BBC reference librarian.

"There's no regular ferry from Iona," said the Scottish Tourist Board, "but you can inquire at Fionnphort."

Preliminaries were conducted by letter, because Beehernz had no telephone. Some of Hopkins's letters were answered, in not very firm handwriting. The contract too came back, signed, but still not pleasing to the festival's accounts manager. "Where's the compensation clause? A specific sum should be named as a guarantee of his appearance . . . They can go missing at any age . . . Stokowski signed a ten-year recording contract at the age of ninety-five . . . It's worse as they get older, they just forget to turn up . . . It needn't be an immense sum . . . What does he live on, anyway?" Hopkins replied that he supposed Beehernz lived on his savings.

Hopkins was more interested in what the old maestro was going to play. Something, certainly, that wouldn't need more than two rehearsals, if possible only one.

"I'd better go and see him myself," he said. This was what he had always had in mind.

He was going to take two other people with him. One was a singer, Mary Lockett. He didn't know her at all well, but she was only just starting on her career and wouldn't refuse — no one ever refused a free trip to Scotland. She had a "white" voice, not really the kind of voice Mahler had liked himself, but she was said to be adaptable. Then he'd take his dogsbody from the festival office, young Fraser. In the evening on the Isle of Reilig they would sit round the piano and let decisions grow. Hopkins couldn't decide whether he expected to find the old man seated, solipsistic, huddled with his past memories, or nervously awaiting visitors, trembling in the overeagerness of welcome. Hopkins wrote to say they would arrive on the twenty-first of May, leaving the car in Oban.

"We'll do well to buy some supplies here," said young Fraser. "Mr. Beehernz will very likely not have much in the house."

They went to Oban's largest supermarket and bought tea, Celebrated Auld Style Shortbread, cold bacon, and, after some hesitation on Hopkins's part, a bottle of whisky. Half a bottle would look too calculated. He didn't know whether Mary Lockett took an occasional drink or not.

"There's always a first time," said Fraser reassuringly.

They crossed to Mull, Fraser and Mary with their backpacks, Hopkins with his discreet travel bag and document case. There was a message for them at Fionnphort, telling them to take the next ferry to Iona and wait for McGregor. At Iona's jetty all the other day-trippers got out and began to walk off briskly, as though drilled, northward towards the cathedral. Time passes more slowly in small places. After what was perhaps three-quarters of an hour, someone who was evidently McGregor came jolting towards them in a Subaru. They'd have to drive over, he said, to the west coast, where he kept his boat at moorings.

Iona is three miles long and one mile wide, and Reilig looked considerably smaller. The blue sky, cloudless that day, burned as if it were as salty as the water below them. There was no sand or white shell beach as you approached, and the rocky shoreline was not impressive, just enough to give you a nasty fall. There was a landing stage with a tarred shed beside it, and a paved trail leading up to a small one-story building of sorts.

"Is that Mr. Beehernz's crofthouse?" Hopkins asked. McGregor replied that it was not a croft, but it was Beehernz's place.

"I imagine he's expecting us," said Hopkins, although he felt it as a kind of weakness to appeal to McGregor, who told them that the door would be open and they'd best go in, but Beehernz might be there or he might be out on his potato patch. When McGregor had seen them safely off the landing stage he disappeared into the shed, which was roofed with corrugated iron.

The front door was shut fast and weeds had grown as high as the lock. The door at the side was open, and led into a dark little hen-kitchen with just enough room for a sink and a cabinet and two disheveled fowls, who ran shrieking into the bright air outside. Fraser and Mary stood awkwardly by the sink, politeness suggesting to them to go no further.

"Beehernz!" Hopkins called. "May we come in?"

I need absolutely to find out what he's really like. This is the opportunity before he comes back.

One step up into the living room, white washed, a clock ticking, no electricity, no radio, a single bed covered with a plaid, an armchair, no books, no bookcase, no scores, no manuscripts. Through into the kitchen, hardly bigger than a cupboard, a paraffin lamp waiting to be filled, a venerable bread crock, and, taking up half the space, a piano, a sad old mission-hall thing, still, a piano. Hopkins lifted the lid and tried the sagging middle C. It was silent. He played up the scale and down. No sound. Next door, the scullery and water closet, fit for an antiquarian.

A disturbance in the hen-kitchen, where the two seedy fowls were rushing in again, reveling in their own panic. Mary and Fraser had just been joined by a third party, an old man who had taken off his gum boots and was now concentrating all his attention on putting on his slippers.

"Ah, you must be . . ." said Hopkins. *But that's quite wrong. I don't want to sound as though I'm the host.*

Beehernz at length said, "I am sorry, but you must let me rest a little. My health, such of it as remains, depends on my doing the same thing at the same time every day."

He advanced with padding steps, a little, light old man, and sat down in the only chair. Hopkins and Fraser sat gingerly on the bed. Mary did not come into the living room. She was still in the hen-kitchen, unfastening the backpacks and taking out the Celebrated Auld Style Shortbread, the cold bacon and the tea. She then began to take down the tin plates from the cabinet. Mary never did anything in a hurry. As she moved about she could be heard singing, just quietly, from the middle of her voice, not paying any particular heed—it was a nursery tune in any case:

"Ich ging im Walde
So für mich hin,
Und nichts zu suchen,
Das war mein Sinn.

In Schatten sah ich
Ein Blumlein stehn—
Where am I to lay out the plates?"

Beehernz was on his feet. "No, no, not now, not yet. Not yet. Let the young people go out for a little while."

"But we brought . . ." Fraser said in unconcealed disappointment.

"For a little while," repeated Beehernz. "Let me explain, Mr. Hopkins. I would prefer Mr. — er — and Miss — er — I would prefer them to go back to Iona with McGregor's boat. Yes, that is what I wish."

"This is rather unexpected. I wrote to you, you remember, to tell you that there would be three of us coming."

Beehernz passed his hands over his forehead and looked out from between them, as though playing some melancholy game.

"Three is too many, Mr. Hopkins, to impose upon me so suddenly."

What's come over him? He may have it in mind to push the two of them over the cliff's edge, two souls for whom I'm responsible to the festival committee.

"I'll go and see where they are."

After all, they couldn't go far. They were sitting on a rocky outcrop, looking westward.

Fraser seemed to be silent, perhaps from hunger. Mary never said much at any time. She was twisting the straw handle of her shopping bag between her fingers. Why did women always have to carry bags about with them?

Hopkins made his explanation. An old man's fancy. They mustn't take it personally.

"How else can we take it?" Fraser asked.

"You'll be able to get accommodation on Iona, perhaps at the abbey."

"Will there be room?"

"Well, perhaps you'll find they've taken some vow not to turn away travelers in an emergency. You must both of you get someone to sign your expenses and keep them in duplicate, of course."

"Surely we ought to say a few words of thanks to Mr. Beehernz," said Fraser.

"No, no, you've nothing to thank him for. You'd better go and put your things together." McGregor, indeed, was advancing up the path, saying that if there was anyone for the return journey, they would want to be getting into the boat.

As the boat ticked away through the calm and sparkling water, Fraser seemed to be shouting something. Sound is always said to carry well over water. This didn't. He'd taken something, or mistaken something. Mary's back was turned, as though on an experience that was over and done with.

When Hopkins got back he found Beehernz methodically chewing the cold bacon. "Sit down, Mr. Hopkins. I eat once a day only, usually in the evening. But if it turns out to be midday, so be it."

And the whisky, what's he done with that? Hopkins realized then what Fraser must have been calling from the boat. He'd taken the bag with the whisky with him, in error, no doubt. The tape recorder was in it, too; Hopkins was left without his standbys, old and new.

"Perhaps you would like to see my potato bed," said Beehernz presently. "I depend on it very extensively. My hens have not laid for nearly a year, although I have not quite lost hope."

They walked up the gently rising ground to the south, past a washing line from which a long-sleeved vest idly flapped, to an open patch of soil surrounded by a low stone wall. Here Beehernz explained his time-honored way of cultivating his crop, describing it as a traditional West Highland method. He didn't bury the seed potatoes, but laid them in rows on the surface and dug trenches between the rows, covering them with earth from the trenches as he did so. McGregor had shown him how to do that—or, to be more accurate, McGregor's father.

"Nothing's come up yet," said Hopkins.

"No, not a green leaf showing." They stood listening to

the gulls crying from every side of them, high up in the deafening blue.

"Why did you try out my piano this morning?" Bee-hernz asked.

You old wretch, you old monster, how do you know I did?

Back in the living room, Hopkins brought the piano stool out of the kitchen and drew it up to the table. Then he opened his document case, moving aside the remnants of the cold food. On this island of Reilig he felt authority leaving him, with no prospect of being replaced by anything else. Authority was scarcely needed in a kingdom of potatoes and seabirds.

I'll begin, he thought, *by calling him by his first name,* then found he had forgotten it. Temporarily of course — he was under stress.

"I respect your privacy, and I'm sure you understand that," he said.

Beehernz replied that he had never considered it at all. "You need two people to respect privacy, or, indeed, to make it necessary."

Hopkins took a selection of documents out of his case. Doing this reassured him. The name was Konrad, of course.

"This is our copy of the original contract. You have had your copy signed and returned to you. It didn't at any time specify what your program was to include. Now, although this wasn't my main object in coming, I've been turning a few thoughts over in my mind, just to see how they strike you." Beehernz simply repeated the word "thoughts" with an inappropriate laugh (it was the first time he had laughed). Hopkins continued, "I take it that you don't, and never did, want to present the monumental Mahler. As I see it, you might begin with some of the early songs — let's say the *Lieder eines fahrenden Gesellen,* the 1884 version, with the piano accompaniment . . ."

Beehernz shook his head slightly with a particularly sweet smile, which, however, wasn't apologetic, rather it dismissed the whole subject.

"Who was that young woman who was here recently?" he asked.

"You mean Mary Lockett. She was here this morning. So, for that matter, was my assistant, Fraser. You told me that you would like them both to leave."

"I assumed that if they came together, they would prefer to leave together."

"That was a total misunderstanding. They're no more than acquaintances."

"A thousand pardons."

He's not of sound mind, reflected Hopkins. *In that case the contract is void anyway.* He said, "Am I to understand, then, that you simply don't want to discuss the subject of Mahler?"

Beehernz smiled still. With a show of determination, Hopkins put another set of papers in front of him, and saw him dutifully bend over them.

After twenty minutes, after which he appeared to be only

at paragraph two, Beehernz looked up and asked, "If I die, or even become seriously ill, before conducting this concert, who will be liable to pay this large sum?" He had understood nothing.

"No one would be liable for that," said Hopkins. "It would be *force majeure.*"

Beehernz put both his hands down flat on the papers, as if to eliminate them from his sight. "Well, I will think about it."

"Couldn't you decide now?"

"Formerly I could have done so, but now I can only think of one thing at a time."

Then what are you thinking about now, you old charlatan, you old crook.

"By the way, don't distress yourself about how you are going to get away from the island. McGregor will be back tomorrow. It will be his regular delivery day, when he brings me my few necessities from Iona."

"What time does he come?"

"He will knock on the door."

"What time?"

"Early, early, at first light. After that I do not expect him back for another two weeks."

Hopkins spent the night in the armchair, which, after years of accommodating Beehernz, resolutely refused to fit anyone else. Since there were no bedclothes in the place beyond the plaid, he slept in his shirt and jacket.

It was still dark when he suggested putting on the kettle. Beehernz, apparently spry and wakeful, told him that he had never possessed a kettle. "That may interest you. We never had one, even when I was a child in Leipzig." He sighed, and went to sleep again. But when the sky grew light, when the unshaven Hopkins had opened the door to McGregor, who said he didn't want tea, thanks, he'd made some in the shed—just as well, Hopkins thought—Beehernz appeared wearing a tattered *Regenhaut* and a wide-brimmed hat. He was ready not only to go out, but to go away.

"I shall accompany you."

"You didn't say anything about this last night."

"I should like to hear that young woman sing again. She cannot have got any further than Iona."

"You sent her away."

"I have changed my mind. I should like to hear her sing again. You see, it is so long since I heard music."

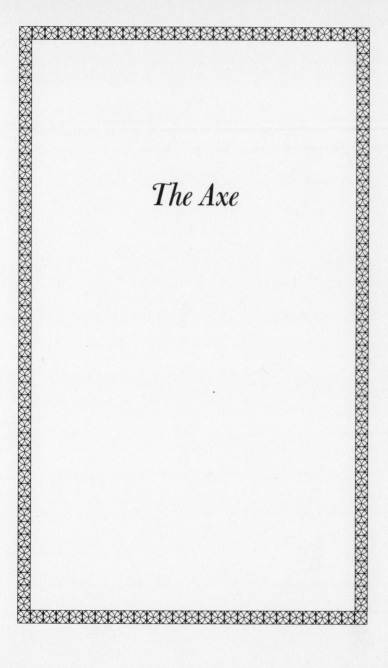

The Axe

$\mathscr{G}$ ... You WILL RECALL that when the planned redundancies became necessary as a result of the discouraging trading figures shown by this small firm—in contrast, so I gather from the Company reports, with several of your other enterprises—you personally deputed to me the task of "speaking" to those who were to be asked to leave. It was suggested to me that if they were asked to resign in order to avoid the unpleasantness of being given their cards, it might be unnecessary for the firm to offer any compensation. Having glanced personally through my staff sheets, you underlined the names of four people, the first being that of my clerical assistant, W. S. Singlebury. Your actual words to me were that he seemed fairly old and could probably be frightened into taking a powder. You were speaking to me in your "democratic" style.

From this point on I feel able to write more freely, it

being well understood, at office-managerial level, that you do not read more than the first two sentences of any given report. You believe that anything which cannot be put into two sentences is not worth attending to, a piece of wisdom which you usually attribute to the late Lord Beaverbrook.

As I question whether you have ever seen Singlebury, with whom this report is mainly concerned, it may be helpful to describe him. He worked for the Company for many more years than myself, and his attendance record was excellent. On Mondays, Wednesdays and Fridays, he wore a blue suit and a green knitted garment with a front zip. On Tuesdays and Thursdays he wore a pair of grey trousers of man-made material which he called "my flannels," and a fawn cardigan. The cardigan was omitted in summer. He had, however, one distinguishing feature, very light blue eyes, with a defensive expression, as though apologizing for something which he felt guilty about, but could not put right. The fact is that he was getting old. Getting old is, of course, a crime of which we grow more guilty every day.

Singlebury had no wife or dependents, and was by no means a communicative man. His room is, or was, a kind of cubbyhole adjoining mine — you have to go through it to get into my room — and it was always kept very neat. About his "things" he did show some mild emotion. They had to be arranged in a certain pattern with respect to his in and out trays, and Singlebury stayed behind for two or three minutes every evening to do this. He also managed to retain every year the complimentary desk calendar sent to us by Dino's, the Italian café on the corner. Singlebury was in fact the only one of my personnel who was always quite certain of the date. To this too his attitude was apologetic. His phrase was, "I'm afraid it's Tuesday."

His work, as was freely admitted, was his life, but the nature of his duties—though they included the post book and the Addressograph—was rather hard to define, having grown round him with the years. I can only say that after he left, I was surprised myself to discover how much he had had to do.

Oddly connected in my mind with the matter of the redundancies is the irritation of the damp in the office this summer and the peculiar smell (not the ordinary smell of damp), emphasized by the sudden appearance of representatives of a firm of damp eliminators who had not been sent for by me, nor is there any record of my having done so. These people simply vanished at the end of the day and have not returned. Another firm, to whom I applied as a result of frequent complaints by the female staff, have answered my letters but have so far failed to call.

Singlebury remained unaffected by the smell. Joining, very much against his usual habit, in one of the too frequent discussions of the subject, he said that he knew what it was: it was the smell of disappointment. For an awkward moment I thought he must have found out by some means that he was going to be asked to go, but he went on to

explain that in 1942 the whole building had been requi-
sitioned by the Admiralty and that relatives had been
allowed to wait or queue there in the hope of getting news
of those missing at sea. The repeated disappointment of
these women, Singlebury said, must have permeated the
building like a corrosive gas. All this was very unlike him. I
make it a point not to encourage anything morbid. Singlebury was quite insistent, and added, as though by way of
proof, that the linoleum in the corridors was Admiralty
issue and had not been replaced since 1942 either. I was
astonished to realize that he had been working in the building for so many years before the present tenancy. I realized
that he must be considerably older than he had given us to
understand. This, of course, will mean that there are wrong
entries on his cards.

The actual notification to the redundant staff passed off
rather better, in a way, than I had anticipated. By that time
everyone in the office seemed inexplicably conversant with
the details, and several of them in fact had gone far beyond their terms of reference—young Patel, for instance,
who openly admits that he will be leaving us as soon as he
can get a better job, taking me aside and telling me that to
such a man as Singlebury dismissal would be like death.
Dismissal is not the right word, I said. But death is, Patel
replied. Singlebury himself, however, took it quietly. Even
when I raised the question of the Company's early retire-
ment pension scheme, which I could not pretend was over-

generous, he said very little. He was generally felt to be in a state of shock. The two girls whom you asked me to speak to were quite unaffected, having already found themselves employment as hostesses at the Dolphinarium near here. Mrs. Horrocks, of Filing, on the other hand, did protest, and was so offensive on the question of severance pay that I was obliged to agree to refer it to a higher level. I consider this as one of the hardest day's work that I have ever done for the Company.

Just before his month's notice (if we are to call it that) was up, Singlebury, to my great surprise, asked me to come home with him one evening for a meal. In all the past years the idea of his having a home, still less asking anyone back to it, had never arisen, and I did not want to go there now. I felt sure, too, that he would want to reopen the matter of compensation, and only a quite unjustified feeling of guilt made me accept. We took the Underground together after work, traveling in the late rush hour to Clapham North, and walked some distance in the rain. His place, when we eventually got to it, seemed particularly inconvenient, the entrance being through a small cleaner's shop. It consisted of one room and a shared toilet on the half-landing. The room itself was tidy, arranged, so it struck me, much on the lines of his cubbyhole, but the window was shut and it was oppressively stuffy. This is where I bury myself, said Singlebury.

There were no cooking arrangements, and he left me

there while he went down to fetch us something ready-to-eat from the Steakorama next to the cleaner's. In his absence I took the opportunity to examine his room, though of course not in an inquisitive or prying manner. I was struck by the fact that none of his small store of stationery had been brought home from the office. He returned with two steaks wrapped in aluminum foil, evidently a special treat in my honor, and afterwards he went out to the landing and made cocoa, a drink which I had not tasted for more than thirty years. The evening dragged rather. In the course of conversation it turned out that Singlebury was fond of reading. There were in fact several issues of a color-printed encyclopedia which he had been collecting as it came out, but unfortunately it had ceased publication after the seventh part. Reading is my hobby, he said. I pointed out that a hobby was rather something that one did with one's hands or in the open air — a relief from the work of the brain. Oh, I don't accept that distinction, Singlebury said. The mind and the body are the same. Well, one cannot deny the connection, I replied. Fear, for example, releases adrenaline, which directly affects the nerves. I don't mean connection, I mean identity, Singlebury said, the mind is the blood. Nonsense, I said, you might just as well tell me that the blood is the mind. It stands to reason that the blood can't think.

I was right, after all, in thinking that he would refer to the matter of the redundancy. This was not till he was seeing me off at the bus stop, when for a moment he turned his grey, exposed-looking face away from me and said that he did not see how he could manage if he really had to go. He stood there like someone who has "tried to give satisfaction" — he even used this phrase, saying that if the expression were not redolent of a bygone age, he would like to feel he had given satisfaction. Fortunately we had not long to wait for the 45 bus.

At the expiry of the month the staff gave a small tea party for those who were leaving. I cannot describe this occasion as a success.

The following Monday I missed Singlebury as a familiar presence and also, as mentioned above, because I had never quite realized how much work he had been taking upon himself. As a direct consequence of losing him I found myself having to stay late — not altogether unwillingly, since although following general instructions I have discouraged overtime, the extra pay in my own case would be instrumental in making ends meet. Meanwhile Singlebury's desk had not been cleared — that is, of the trays, pencil sharpener and complimentary calendar, which were, of course, office property. The feeling that he would come back — not like Mrs. Horrocks, who has rung up and called round incessantly, but simply come back to work out of habit and through not knowing what else to do — was very strong, without being openly mentioned. I myself half expected and dreaded it, and I had mentally prepared two or three lines of argument in order to persuade him, if he did come, not to try it again. Nothing happened, however, and on the Thursday I personally removed the "things" from the cubbyhole into my own room.

Meanwhile, in order to dispel certain quite unfounded rumors, I thought it best to issue a notice for general circulation, pointing out that if Mr. Singlebury should turn out to have taken any unwise step, and if in consequence any inquiry should be necessary, we should be the first to hear about it from the police. I dictated this to our only permanent typist, who immediately said, Oh, he would never do that. He would never cause any unpleasantness like bringing police into the place, he'd do all he could to avoid that. I did not encourage any further discussion, but I asked my wife, who is used to social work, to call round at Singlebury's place in Clapham North and find out how he was. She did not have very much luck. The people in the cleaner's shop knew, or thought they knew, that he was away, but they had not been sufficiently interested to ask where he was going.

On Friday young Patel said he would be leaving, as the damp and the smell were affecting his health. The damp is certainly not drying out in this seasonably warm weather.

I also, as you know, received another invitation on the Friday, at very short notice, in fact no notice at all; I was told to come to your house in Suffolk Park Gardens that evening for drinks. I was not unduly elated, having been asked once before, after I had done rather an awkward small job for you. In our Company, justice must not only not be done, it must be seen not to be done. The food was quite nice; it came from your Caterers Grade 3. I spent most of the evening talking to Ted Hollow, one of the area sales managers. I did not expect to be introduced to your wife, nor was I. Towards the end of the evening you spoke to me for three minutes in the small room with a green marble floor and matching wallpaper leading to the ground-floor toilets. You asked me if everything was all right, to which I replied, All right for whom? You said that nobody's fault was nobody's funeral. I said that I had tried to give satisfaction. Passing on towards the washbasins, you told me with seeming cordiality to be careful and watch it when I had had mixed drinks.

I would describe my feeling at this point as resentment, and I cannot identify exactly the moment when it passed into unease. I do know that I was acutely uneasy as I crossed the hall and saw two of your domestic staff, a man and a woman, holding my coat, which I had left in the lobby, and apparently trying to brush it. Your domestic staff all appear to be of foreign extraction, and I personally feel sorry for them and do not grudge them a smile at the oddly assorted guests. Then I saw they were not smiling at my coat but that they seemed to be examining their fingers and looking at me earnestly and silently, and the collar or shoulders of my coat were covered with blood. As I came up to them, although they were still both absolutely silent, the illusion or impression passed, and I put on my coat and left the house in what I hope was a normal manner.

I now come to the present time. The feeling of uneasiness which I have described as making itself felt in your house has not diminished during this past weekend, and partly to take my mind off it and partly for the reasons I have given, I decided to work overtime again tonight, Monday the twenty-third. This was in spite of the fact that the damp smell had become almost a stench, as of something putrid, which must have affected my nerves to some extent, because when I went out to get something to eat at Dino's I left the lights on, both in my own office and in the entrance hall. I mean that for the first time since I began to work for the Company I left them on deliberately. As I walked to the corner I turned and saw the two solitary lights looking somewhat forlorn in contrast to the glitter of the Arab-American Mutual Loan Corporation opposite. After my meal I felt absolutely reluctant to go back to the building, and wished then that I had not given way to the impulse to leave the lights on, but since I had done so and they must be turned off, I had no choice.

As I stood in the empty hallway I could hear the numerous creakings, settlings and faint tickings of an old building, possibly associated with the plumbing system. The lifts for reasons of economy do not operate after 6:30 P.M., so I began to walk up the stairs. After one flight I felt a strong creeping tension in the nerves of my back such as any of us feels when there is danger from behind; one might say that the body was thinking for itself on these occasions. I did not look round, but simply continued upwards as rapidly as I could. At the third floor, I paused, and could hear footsteps coming patiently up behind me. This was not a surprise; I had been expecting them all evening.

Just at the door of my own office — or rather of the cubbyhole, for I have to pass through that — I turned and saw at the end of the dim corridor what I had also expected, Singlebury, advancing towards me with his unmistakable shuffling step. My first reaction was a kind of bewilderment as to why he, who had been such an excellent timekeeper, so regular day by day, should become a creature of the night. He was wearing the blue suit. This I could make out by its familiar outline, but it was not till he came halfway down the corridor towards me, and reached the patch of light falling through the window from the street, that I saw that he was not himself — I mean that his head was nodding, or rather swiveling, irregularly from side to side. It crossed my mind that Singlebury was drunk. I had never known him drunk or indeed seen him take anything to drink, even at the office Christmas party, but one cannot estimate the effect that trouble will have upon a man. I began to think what steps I should take in this situation. I turned on the light in his cubbyhole as I went through and waited at the entrance of my own office. When he appeared in the outer doorway I saw that I had not been correct about the reason for the odd movement of the head. The throat was cut from ear to ear so that the head was nearly severed from the shoulders. It was this which had given the impression of nodding, or rather lolling. As he walked into his cubbyhole Singlebury raised both hands and tried to steady the head as though conscious that something was wrong. The eyes were thickly filmed over, as one sees in the carcasses in a butcher's shop.

I shut and locked my door, and not wishing to give way to nausea, or lose all control of myself, I sat down at my desk. My work was waiting for me as I had left it — it was the file on the matter of the damp elimination — and, there not being anything else to do, I tried to look through it. On the other side of the door I could hear Singlebury sit down also, and then try the drawers of the table, evidently look-ing for the "things" without which he could not start work. After the drawers had been tried, one after another, several times, there was almost total silence.

The present position is that I am locked in my own office and would not, no matter what you offered me, indeed I could not, go out through the cubbyhole and pass what is sitting at the desk. The early cleaners will not be here for seven hours and forty-five minutes. I have passed the time so far as best I could in writing this report. One consideration strikes me. If what I have next door is a visi-tant which should not be walking but buried in the earth, then its wound cannot bleed, and there will be no stream of blood moving slowly under the whole width of the communicating door. However, I am sitting at the moment with my back to the door, so that, without turning round, I have no means of telling whether it has done so or not.

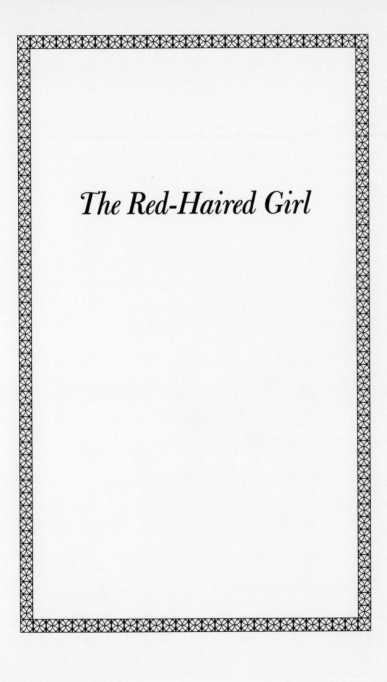

The Red-Haired Girl

SG HACKETT, Holland, Parsons, Charrington and Dubois all studied in Paris, in the atelier of Vincent Bonvin. Dubois, although his name sounded French, wasn't, and didn't speak any either. None of them did except Hackett.

In the summer of 1882 they made up a party to go to Brittany. That was because they admired Bastien-Lepage, which old Bonvin definitely didn't, and because they wanted somewhere cheap, somewhere with characteristic types, absolutely natural, busy with picturesque occupations and, above all, plein air. "Your work cannot be really good unless you have caught a cold doing it," said Hackett.

They were poor enough, but they took a certain quantity of luggage—only the necessities. Their canvases needed rigging like small craft putting out of harbor, and the artists themselves, for plein air work, had brought overcoats, knickerbockers, gaiters, boots, wide-awakes, broad straw hats for sunny days. They tried, to begin with, St. Briac-sur-Mer, which had been recommended to them in Paris, but it didn't suit. On, then, to Palourde, on the coast near Cancale. All resented the time spent moving about. It wasn't in the spirit of the thing — they were artists, not sightseers.

At Palourde, although it looked, and was, larger than St. Briac, there was, if anything, less room. The Palourdais had never come across artists before, considered them as rich rather than poor, and wondered why they did not go to St. Malo. Holland, Parsons, Charrington and Dubois, how-ever, each found a room of sorts. What about their posses-sions? There were sail lofts and potato cellars in Palourde, but, it seemed, not an inch of room to spare. Their clothes, books and painting materials had to go in some boats pulled up above the foreshore, awaiting repairs. They were covered with a piece of tarred sailcloth and roped down. Half the morning would have to be spent getting out what was wanted. Hackett, as interpreter, was obliged to ask whether there was any risk of their being stolen. The reply was that no one in Palourde wanted such things.

It was agreed that Hackett should take what appeared to be the only room in the constricted Hotel du Port. "Right under the rafters," he wrote to his intended, "a bed, a chair, a basin, a broc of cold water brought up once a day, no view from the window, but I shan't of course paint in my room anyway. I have propped up the canvases I brought with me against the wall. That gives me the sensation of having done something. The food, so far, you wouldn't approve of. Black porridge, later on pieces of black porridge left over from the morning and fried, fish soup with onions, onion soup with fish. The thing is to understand these people well, try to share their devotion to onions, and above all to secure a good model" — he decided not to add "who must be a young girl, otherwise I haven't much chance of any of the London exhibitions."

The Hotel du Port was inconveniently placed at the top of the village. It had no restaurant, but Hackett was told that he could be served, if he wanted it, at half past six o'clock. The ground floor was taken up with the bar, so this service would be in a very small room at the back, opening off the kitchen.

After Hackett had sat for some time at a narrow table covered with rose-patterned oilcloth, the door opened sufficiently for a second person to edge into the room. It was a red-haired girl, built for hard use and hard wear, who without speaking put down a bowl of fish soup. She and the soup between them filled the room with a sharp, cloudy odor, not quite disagreeable, but it wasn't possible for her to get in and out, concentrating always on not spilling anything, without knocking the back of the chair and the door itself, first with her elbows, then with her rump. The spoons and the saltbox on the table trembled as though in a railway carriage. Then the same maneuver again, this time bringing a loaf of dark bread and a carafe of cider. No more need to worry after that; there was no more to come.

"I think I've found rather a jolly-looking model already," Hackett told the others. They, too, had not done so badly. They had set up their easels on the quay; been asked, as far as they could make out, to move them farther away from the moorings; done so "with a friendly smile," said Charrington — "we find that goes a long way." They hadn't risked asking anyone to model for them, just started some sea pieces between the handfuls of wind and rain. "We might come up to the hotel tonight and dine with you. There's nothing but fish soup in our digs."

Hackett discouraged them.

The hotelier's wife, when he had made the right preliminary inquiries to her about the red-haired girl, had answered — as she did on all subjects — largely with silences. He didn't learn who her parents were, or even her family name. Her given name was Annik. She worked an all-day job at the Hotel du Port, but she had one and a half hours free after her lunch, and if she wanted to spend that time being drawn or painted, well, there were no objections. Not in the hotel, however, where, as he could see, there was no room.

"I paint en plein air," said Hackett.

"You'll find plenty of that."

"I shall pay her, of course."

"You must make your own arrangements."

He spoke to the girl at dinner, during the few moments when she was conveniently trapped. When she had quite skillfully allowed the door to shut behind her and, soup dish in hand, was recovering her balance, he said: "Anny, I want to ask you something."

"I'm called Annik," she said. It was the first time he had heard her speak.

"All the girls are called that. I shall call you Anny. I've spoken about you to the patronne."

"Yes, she told me."

Anny was a heavy breather, and the whole tiny room seemed to expand and deflate as she stood pondering.

"I shall want you to come to the back door of the hotel, I mean the back steps down to the Rue de Dol. Let us say tomorrow, at twelve forty-five."

"I don't know about the forty-five," she said. "I can't be sure about that."

"How do you usually know the time?" She was silent. He thought it was probably a matter of pride and she did not want to agree to anything too easily. But possibly she couldn't tell the time. She might be stupid to the degree of idiocy.

The Hotel du Port had no courtyard. Like every other house in the street, it had a flight of stone steps to adapt to the change of level. After lunch the shops shut for an hour and the women of Palourde sat or stood, according to their age, on the top step and knitted or did crochet. They didn't wear costume anymore, they wore white linen caps and jackets, long skirts, and, if they weren't going far, carpet slippers.

Anny was punctual to the minute. "I shall want you to stand quite still on the top step, with your back to the door. I've asked them not to open it."

Anny also was wearing carpet slippers. "I can't just stand here doing nothing."

He allowed her to fetch her crochet. Give a little, take a little. He was relieved, possibly a bit disappointed, to find how little interest they caused in the Rue de Dol. He was used to being watched, quite openly, over his shoulder, as if he were giving a comic performance. Here even the children didn't stop to look.

"They don't care about our picture," he said, trying to amuse her. He would have liked a somewhat gentler expression. Certainly she was not a beauty. She hadn't the white skin of the dreamed-of red-haired girl. In fact, her face and neck were covered with a faint but noticeable hairy down, as though proof against all weathers.

"How long will it take?" she asked.

"I don't know. As God disposes! An hour will do for today."

"And then you'll pay me?" "No," he said, "I shan't do that. I shall pay you when the whole thing's finished. I shall keep a record of the time you've worked, and if you like you can keep one as well."

As he was packing up his box of charcoals he added, "I shall want to make a few color notes tomorrow, and I should like you to wear a red shawl." It seemed that she hadn't one. "But you could borrow one, my dear. You could borrow one, since I ask you particularly."

She looked at him as though he were an imbecile.

"You shouldn't have said 'since I ask you particularly,'" Parsons told him that evening. "That will have turned her head."

"It can't have done," said Hackett.

"Did you call her 'my dear'?"

"I don't know, I don't think so."

"I've noticed you say 'particularly' with a peculiar intonation, which may well have become a matter of habit," said Parsons, nodding sagely.

This is driving me crazy, thought Hackett. He began to feel a division which he had never so much as imagined of in Paris between himself and his fellow students. They had been working all day, having managed to rent a disused and indeed almost unusable shed on the quay. It had once been part of the market where the fishermen's wives did the triage, sorting out the catch by size. Hackett, as before, had done the interpreting. He had plenty of time, since Anny could only be spared for such short intervals. But at least he had been true to his principles. Holland, Parsons, Charrington and Dubois weren't working in the open air at all. Difficulties about models forgotten, they were sketching each other in the shed. The background of

Palourde's not very picturesque jetty could be dashed in later.

Anny appeared promptly for the next three days to stand, with her crochet, on the back steps. Hackett didn't mind her blank expression, having accepted from the first that she was never likely to smile. The red shawl, though —that hadn't appeared. He could, perhaps, buy one in St. Malo. He ached for the contrast between the copper-colored hair and the scarlet shawl. But he felt it wrong to introduce something from outside Palourde.

"Anny, I have to tell you that you've disappointed me."

"I told you I had no red shawl."

"You could have borrowed one."

Charrington, who was supposed to understand women, and even to have had a great quarrel with Parsons about some woman or other, only said, "She can't borrow what isn't there. I've been trying ever since we came here to borrow a decent tin opener. I've tried to make it clear that I'd give it back."

Best to leave the subject alone. But the moment Anny turned up next day he found himself saying, "You could borrow one from a friend, that was what I meant."

"I haven't any friends," said Anny. Hackett paused in the business of lighting his pipe. "An empty life for you, then, Anny."

"You don't know what I want," she said, very low.

"Oh, everybody wants the same things. The only difference is what they will do to get them."

"You don't know what I want, and you don't know what I feel," she said, still in the same mutter. There was, however, a faint note of something more than the contradiction that came so naturally to her, and Hackett was a good-natured man.

"I'm sorry I said you disappointed me, Anny. The truth is I find it rather a taxing business, standing here drawing in the street."

"I don't know why you came here in the first place. There's nothing here, nothing at all. If it's oysters you want, they're better at Cancale. There's nothing here to tell one morning from another, except to see if it's raining . . . Once they brought in three drowned bodies, two men and a boy, a whole boat's crew, and laid them out on the tables in the fish market, and you could see blood and water running out of their mouths . . . You can spend your whole life here, wash, pray, do your work, and all the time you might just as well not have been born."

She was still speaking so that she could scarcely be heard. The passersby went unnoticing down Palourde's badly paved street. Hackett felt disturbed. It had never occurred to him that she would speak, without prompting, at such length.

"I've received a telegram from Paris," said Parsons, who was standing at the shed door. "It's taken its time about getting here. They gave it me at the post office."

"What does it say?" asked Hackett, feeling it was likely to be about money.

"Well, that he's coming—Bonvin, I mean. 'As is my custom every summer, I am touring the coasts.' It's a kind of informal inspection, you see. 'Expect me, then, on the twenty-seventh for dinner at the Hotel du Port.'"

"It's impossible." Parsons suggested that, since Dubois had brought his banjo with him, they might get up some kind of impromptu entertainment. But he had to agree that one didn't associate old Bonvin with entertainment.

He couldn't, surely, be expected from Paris before six. But when they arrived, all of them except Hackett carrying their portfolios, at the hotel's front door, they recognized, from the moment it opened, the voice of Bonvin. Hackett looked round and felt his head swim. The bar —dark, faded, pickled in its own long-standing odors, crowded with stools and barrels, with the air of being older than Palourde, as though Palourde had been built round it without daring to disturb it—was swept and empty now except for a central table and chairs such as Hackett had never seen in the hotel. At the head of the table sat old Bonvin. "Sit down, gentlemen! I am your host!" The everyday malicious dry voice, but a different Bonvin, in splendid seaside dress, a yellow waistcoat, a cravat. Palourde was indifferent to artists, but Bonvin had imposed himself as a professor.

"They are used to me here. They keep a room for me which I think is not available to other guests, and they are always ready to take a little trouble for me when I come."

The artists sat meekly down while the patronne herself

served them with a small glass of greenish-white Muscadet.

"I am your host," repeated Bonvin. "I can only say that I am delighted to see pupils, for the first time, in Palourde, but I assure you I have others as far away as Corsica. Once a teacher, always a teacher! I sometimes think it is a passion which outlasts even art itself."

In Paris, they had all assured each other that old Bonvin was incapable of teaching anything. Time spent in his atelier was squandered. But here, in the strangely transformed bar of the Hotel du Port, with a quite inadequate drink in front of them, they felt overtaken by destiny. The patronne shut and locked the front door to keep out the world who might disturb the professor. Bonvin — not, after all, looking so old — called upon them to show their portfolios.

Hackett had to excuse himself to go up to his room and fetch the four drawings which he had made so far. He felt it an injustice that he had to show his things last.

Bonvin asked him to hold them up one by one, then to lay them out on the table. To Hackett he spoke magniloquently in French.

"Yes, they are bad," he said, "but, Monsieur Hackett, they are bad for two distinct reasons. In the first place, you should not draw the view from the top of a street if you cannot manage the perspective, which even a child, following simple mechanical rules, can do. The relationship in scale of the main figure to those lower down is quite, quite wrong. But there is something else amiss.

"You are an admirer, I know, of Bastien-Lepage, who has

said, 'There is nothing really lasting, nothing that will en-
dure, except the sincere expression of the actual conditions
of life.' Conditions in the potato patch, in the hayfield, at
the washtub, in the open street! That is pernicious nonsense. Look at this girl of yours. Evidently she is not a professional model, for she doesn't know how to hold herself.
I see you have made a note that the color of the hair is red,
but that is the only thing I know about her. She's standing
against the door like a beast waiting to be put back in its
stall. It's your intention, I am sure, to do the finished version in the same way, in the dust of the street. Well, your
picture will say nothing and it will be nothing. It is only in
the studio that you can bring out the heart of the subject,
and that is what we are sent into this world to do, Monsieur
Hackett, to paint the experiences of the heart."

—Gibbering dotard, you can talk till your teeth fall out.
I shall go on precisely as I have been doing, even if I can
only paint her for an hour and a quarter a day.—An evening of nameless embarrassment, with Hackett's friends
coughing, shuffling, eating noisily, asking questions to
which they knew the answers, and telling anecdotes of
which they forgot the endings. Anny had not appeared,
evidently she was considered unworthy. The patronne
came in again, bringing not soup but the very height of
Brittany's grand-occasion cuisine, a fricassee of chicken.
Who would have thought there were chickens in Palourde?

*

Hackett woke in what he supposed were the small hours. So far he had slept dreamlessly in Palourde, had never so much as lighted his bedside candle. — Probably, he thought, Bonvin made the same unpleasant speech wherever he went. The old impostor was drunk with power, not with anything else, only half a bottle of Muscadet and, later, a bottle of Gros-Plant among the six of them. — The sky had begun to thin and pale. It came to him that what had been keeping him awake was not an injustice of Bonvin's, but of his own. What had been the experiences of Anny's heart?

Bonvin, with his dressing cases and book boxes, left early. The horse omnibus stopped once a week in the little Place François-René de Chateaubriand, at the entrance to the village. Having made his formal farewells, Bonvin caught the omnibus. Hackett was left in good time for his appointment with Anny.

She did not come that day, nor the next day, nor the day after. On the first evening he was served by the bootboy, pitifully worried about getting in and out of the door, on the second by the hotel laundrywoman, on the third by the patronne. "Where is Anny?" The patronne did not answer. For that in itself Hackett was prepared, but he tried again. "Is she ill?" "No, not ill." "Has she taken another job?" "No." He was beginning, he realized, in the matter of this plain and sullen girl, to sound like an anxious lover. "Shall I see her again?" He got no answer.

Had she drowned herself? The question reared up in his mind like a savage dog getting up from its sleep. She had hardly seemed to engage herself enough with life, hardly seemed to take enough interest in it to wish no more of it. Boredom, though, and the withering sense of insignificance can bring one as low as grief. He had felt the breath of it at his ear when Bonvin had told him — for that was what it came to — that there was no hope of his becoming an artist. Anny was stupid, but no one is too stupid to despair.

There was no police station in Palourde, and if Anny were truly drowned, they would say nothing about it at the Hotel du Port. Hackett had been in enough small hotels to know that they did not discuss anything that was bad for business. The red-haired body might drift anywhere, might be washed ashore anywhere between Pointe du Grouin and Cap Prehel.

That night it was the laundrywoman's turn to dish up the fish soup. Hackett thought of confiding in her, but did not need to. She said to him, "You mustn't keep asking the patronne about Anny, it disturbs her." Anny, it turned out, had been dismissed for stealing from the hotel — some money and a watch. "You had better have a look through your things," the laundrywoman said, "and see there's nothing missing. One often doesn't notice till a good while afterwards."

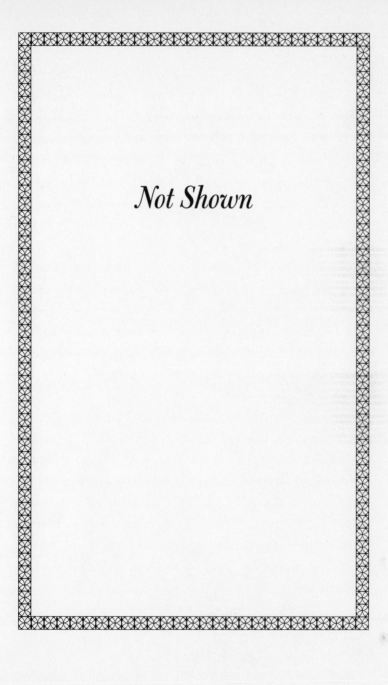

Not Shown

LADY P lived at Tailfirst, which was not shown to the public. Fothergill was the resident administrator, or dogsbody, at Tailfirst Farm, which was shown April 1 to end October, Mon, Wed, Sat: no coach parties, no backpackers, guide dogs by arrangement, WC, small shop. It was the old Home Farm, sympathetically rebuilt in red brick between 1892 and 1894 by Philip Webb (a good example of his later manner), the small herb and lavender garden possibly suggested by Gertrude Jekyll. The National Trust had steadfastly refused to take it over; still, they can make mistakes, like the rest of us.

"Now Fothergill, as to the room stewards," said Lady P, returning with frighteningly renewed energies from the Maldives.

"The ladies . . ."

"The Trust calls them room stewards . . ."

"Two of them, of course, are your own recommendations — Mrs. Feare, who was at the Old Pottery Shop until it closed, and Mrs. Twine, who was dinner lady at the village school."

"Until that closed. Faithful souls both."

"I'm sure they are, and that is my great difficulty."

"Don't confuse yourself with detail. You must treasure Twine and Feare, and dispense with Mrs. Horrabin."

"I should very much like to do that," said Fothergill.

Lady P looked at him sharply. "I'm told in the village that you only engaged her last Wednesday. Now, in any group of employees, and perhaps particularly with low-paid employees, a dominating figure creates discord."

"Do you know Mrs. Horrabin well, Lady P?" asked Fothergill.

"Of course not. I've been obliged to meet her, I think twice, on my recreation committee. She comes from the industrial estate at Battisford, as you ought to know."

"I do know it."

"You don't look well, you know, Fothergill. When you came into the room I thought, The man doesn't look well. Are you still worrying about anything?"

He collected himself for a moment. "In what way am I to get rid of Mrs. Horrabin?"

"I'm sure you don't want me to tell you how to do your job," said Lady P.

"I do want you to tell me."

Fothergill lived in one of the attics (not shown) at the Farm, on a salary so small that it was difficult to see how he had survived for the past year. Undoubtedly there was something not quite right about him, or by the time he was fifty-six — if that was his real age — he would be married (perhaps he had been), and he would certainly by now have found some better employment. Lady P, who found it better in every way not to leave such things to her husband, had drafted the advertisement which was specifically aimed at applicants with something not quite right about them, who would come cheap: "Rent free accommodation, remote, peaceful situation, ample free time, suit writer." Fothergill wasn't a writer, but then he soon discovered there wasn't much free time either.

"I do want you to tell me," he repeated.

He had known very little about architecture when he came, nothing about tile hanging, weatherboarding, lead box-guttering or late-Victorian electrical fittings, and he had never heard of Philip Webb. He learned these things between maintaining the garden, the old Land Rover and the still older petrol mower. But the home-made damson cordials were manufactured and supplied by a Pakistani-owned firm in Sheffield, no trouble there, and to his surprise, Mrs. Feare and Mrs. Twine had agreed to come. "You're a novelty for them," said the man who came to clean out the cesspit. It was gratifying to Fothergill to be described as a novelty.

So far there had been worryingly few visitors, but he disposed carefully of his small force. Mrs. Twine couldn't stand for too long, and was best off in the dining room where there was a solid table to lean against; on the other hand, she was sharper than Mrs. Feare, who let people linger in the conservatory and nick the tomatoes.

Mrs. Feare was more at home in the shop with the fudge and postcards, and her ten-year-old son biked up after school to work out the day's VAT on his calculator. Mrs. Twine also fancied herself in the shop, but had no son to offer. Fothergill hurried about between the garden, the white-painted drawing room and the cash desk. Each day solved itself, by closing time, without complaints. A remote, peaceful situation.

Mrs. Horrabin had driven up to the front door of the Farm at 9 A.M. last Tuesday. To avoid shouting out of the bedroom window he had come downstairs, unbarred, unlocked and unopened. "The house is not shown today, madam. Can I help you at all?"

"We'll see," said Mrs. Horrabin.

Hugely, beigely, she got out of her Sunny, and with a broad white smile told him her name.

"I've decided to take over here."

"I'm afraid there are no vacancies."

"Shirley Twine won't be coming back after the end of this week."

"She said nothing . . ."

"She'll take a hint."

"Mrs. Feare . . ."

"I'll give her a hint as well. They won't either of them break their hearts over it. They can get another little job easily enough." She stared at him boldly and unpeaceably. "Some can, some can't."

Although from long habit Fothergill pretended not to understand her, he was in no way surprised. He was pretty sure he had never met Mrs. Horrabin before, but that didn't mean that through one of life's thousand unhappy coincidences she might not know something unacceptable about him. He had lived in so many places, and so often left them in a hurry.

"Didn't you once work as a credit manager in Basingstoke?" she asked now. "An uncle of mine lives there."

She belonged to the tribe of torturers. Why pretend they don't exist?

"You have it in mind," he said, "to take away my last chance."

Mrs. Horrabin ignored this. "I know what's wrong with this place. You've got these two old boilers standing in the corners of the rooms and they make people afraid to come in at all. In any case they don't particularly want to look at what's on show, they want to have a good poke around. They want to see the bedrooms and the john."

In default of a decent piece of rope Fothergill had placed

a handwritten card, PRIVATE, on the front stairs. Mrs. Horrabin actually trod on it — visitors wearing stiletto heels not admitted — on her way up. In rage and disgust he followed her into the never-used, pomegranate-papered front bedroom where, marching in, she dragged down the blinds.

"It isn't necessary to restrict the light in here," he said, clinging to his professional status. "There are no watercolors."

"I like them down. Just for half an hour or so."

She sat down on the double bed, whose box-springs reverberated, and took off her jacket. She was wearing a very low-necked blouse with machine embroidery. "I don't believe you know what to do next," she said.

Fothergill cried, "It's only twenty past nine in the morning." It was not quite what he had meant to say. He went on, "You're making a grotesque mistake."

"Well, perhaps I am, we'll have to see," said Mrs. Horrabin. "At least, though, you've got your own teeth. You can't go wrong about that, you can always catch the gleam of dentures. Anyway, the choice isn't so wide round here."

From her great beige bag, which she had never so far left hold of, a great monotonous chirp began, like a demented pipit.

"That'll be Mr. Horrabin outside in your drive." She opened her bag and took out her mobile phone. "Tweety calling Bub . . ."

"Your husband knows you're here?"

"He always knows where I am. He isn't against my

enjoying myself, he stretches a point there, but he likes to feel included."

"Included in what way?"

"He's an area salesman for alternative medicines . . . He wants me at home, it seems, so I'm letting you off for this morning . . . But I'll be back tomorrow. We'll be able to manage quite well between us."

He shouted, "You have robbed me of Mrs. Feare and Mrs. Twine, you have taken away my peace of mind, and what's worse I find you completely unattractive." Or perhaps he had never said the words aloud, since Mrs. Horrabin was standing self-approvingly in front of the cheval glass with the calm smile of the powerful, smoothing the shoulders of her jacket.

While Fothergill allowed himself to think backwards into the trap of his mind, Lady P had been talking on, passing to many other topics, and now gracefully returned. He mustn't blame himself too much, she said, for the disappointing figures. Apart from the fact that they didn't do teas, the great drawback was that nothing interesting had ever happened at Tailfirst Farm. Not a murder, she didn't mean that, although it would certainly create some interest, but perhaps some sad and unexpected accident . . . She laughed a little, to show that a joke had been intended, but saw that Fothergill had been quite prepared to agree with her. He hasn't much spirit, she thought. Probably he never thinks about anything except keeping his job.

At Hiruharama

MR. TANNER was anxious to explain how it was that he had a lawyer in the family, so that when they all decided to sell up and quit New Zealand there had been someone they could absolutely trust with the legal business. That meant that he had to say something about his grandfather, who had been an orphan from Stamford in Lincolnshire and was sent out to a well-to-do family north of Auckland, supposedly as an apprentice, but it turned out that he was to be more or less of a servant: he cleaned the knives, saw to the horses, waited at table and chopped the wood. On an errand to a dry goods store in Auckland he met Kitty, Mr. Tanner's grandmother. She had come out from England as a governess, and she too found she was really wanted as a servant. She was sixteen, and Tanner asked her to wait for three years while he saved his wages, and then to marry him. All this was at a Methodist social, say a couple of weeks later. "What family have you got back home?" Kitty asked him. Tanner replied just the one sister. Younger or older? Older. She probably thinks I'm a skilled craftsman by now. She probably reckons I'm made. — Haven't you sent word to her lately? — Not lately. — Best write to her now, anyway, said Kitty, and tell her how it is between us. I should be glad to have a new relation, I haven't many. — I'll think it over, he said. Kitty realized then that he could neither read nor write.

They had to start in a remote country place. The land round Auckland at that time was ten shillings an acre, a third of the price going to build the new churches and schools, but where Tanner and Kitty went, north of Awanui, there weren't any churches and schools, and it was considerably cheaper. They didn't have to buy their place, it had been left deserted, and yet it had something you could give a thousand pounds for and not get, and that was a standpipe giving constant clear water from an underground well. But whoever lived there had given up, because of the loneliness and because it was such poor country. Don't picture a shack, though. There were two rooms, one with a stove and one with a bedstead, and a third one at the back for a vegetable store. Tanner grew root vegetables and went into Awanui twice a week with the horse and dray. Kitty stayed behind, because they'd taken on two hundred chickens and a good few pigs.

Tanner turned over in his mind what he'd say to his wife

when she told him she was going to have a child. When she did tell him, which wasn't for another two years or so, by the way, he didn't hear her at first, because a northerly was blowing and neither of them could expect to hear each other. When he did catch what she was saying, he hitched up and drove into Awanui. The doctor was at his midday dinner, which he took at a boardinghouse higher up the main street. When he got back and into his consulting room Tanner asked him what were the life statistics of the North Island.

"Do you mean the death statistics?" the doctor asked.

"They'll do just as well," said Tanner.

"No one dies here except from drink or drowning. Out of three thousand people in Taranaki Province there hasn't been a single funeral in the last sixteen months and only twenty-four sick and infirm. You may look upon me as a poor man."

"What about women in childbirth?" asked Tanner.

The doctor didn't have any figures for women dying in childbirth, but he looked sharply at Tanner and asked him when his child was due.

"You don't know, of course," the doctor said. "Well, don't ask me if it's going to be twins. Nature didn't intend us to know that." He began to write in his notebook. "Where are you living?"

"It's off the road to Houhora. You turn off to the right after twelve miles."

[*109*]

"What's it called?"

"Hiruharama."

"Don't know it. That's not a Maori name."

"I think it means Jerusalem," said Tanner.

"Are there any other women about the place?"

"No."

"I mean someone who could come in and look after things while your wife's laid up. Who's your nearest neighbor?" Tanner told him there was no one except a man called Brinkman, who came over sometimes. He was about nine or ten miles off at Stony Loaf.

"And he has a wife?"

"No, he hasn't, that's what he complains about. You couldn't ask a woman to live out there."

"You can ask a woman to live anywhere," said the doctor. "He's a crank, I daresay."

"He's a dreamer," Tanner replied. "I should term Brinkman a dreamer."

"I was thinking in terms of washing the sheets, that sort of thing. If there's no one else, can you manage about the house yourself for a few days?"

"I can do anything about the house," said Tanner.

"You don't drink?"

Tanner shook his head, wondering if the doctor did. He asked if he shouldn't bring his wife with him for a consultation next time he drove over to Awanui. The doctor looked out of his window at the bone-shaking old dray with its iron-rimmed wheels. "Don't."

He tore the prescription out of his notebook. "Get this for your wife. It's calcium water. When you want me to come, you'll have to send for me. But don't let that worry you. Often by the time I arrive I'm not needed."

Other patients had arrived and were sitting on the wooden benches on the verandah. Some had empty medicine bottles for a refill. There was a man with his right arm strapped up, several kids with their mothers, and a woman who looked well enough but seemed to be in tears for some reason or other. — Well, you see life in the townships.

Tanner went over to the post office, where there was free pen and ink if you wanted it, and wrote a letter to his sister. — But wait a minute, surely he couldn't read or write? Evidently by that time he could. Mr. Tanner's guess was that although Kitty was a quiet girl, very quiet, she'd refused to marry him until he'd got the hang of it. — Tanner wrote: My darling old sister. Well, it's come to pass and either a girl or a boy will be added unto us. It would be a help if you could send us a book on the subject. We have now a hundred full-grown hens and a further hundred at point of lay, and a good stand of potatoes. — After mailing the letter he bought soap, thread, needles, canned fish, tea and sugar. When he drove out of Awanui he stopped at the last homestead, where he knew a man called Parrish who kept racing pigeons. Some of them, in fact, were just arriving back at their loft. Parrish had cut the entrances to the nests down very small, and every time a bird got home it had to squeeze past a bell on a string so that the tinkling sound gave warning. They were all Blue Checkers, the only kind, Parrish declared, that a sane man would want to keep. Tanner explained his predicament and asked for the loan of two birds. Parrish didn't mind, because Hiruharama, Tanner's place, was on a more or less direct line from Awanui to Te Paki station, and that was the line his pigeons flew.

"If you'd have lived over the other way I couldn't have helped you," Parrish said.

A Maori boy took the young birds out as soon as they were four months old and tossed them at three miles, ten miles, twenty miles, always in the same direction, north-northwest of Awanui.

"As long as they can do fifteen miles," said Tanner.

"They can do two hundred and fifty."

"How long will it take them to do fifteen miles?"

"Twenty minutes in clear weather," said Parrish.

The Maori boy picked out two birds and packed them into a wicker hamper, which Tanner wedged into the driver's seat of the dray.

"Have you got them numbered in some way?" Tanner asked.

"I don't need to. I know them all," said Parrish.

He added that they would need rock salt, so Tanner drove back into the town once more to buy the rock salt and a sack of millet. By the time he got to Hiruharama the clear night sky was pressing in on every side. I ought to have taken you with me, he told Kitty. She said she had been all right. He hadn't, though; he'd been worried. You mean you've forgotten something at the stores, said Kitty. Tanner went out to the dray and fetched the pigeons, still shifting about and conferring quietly in their wicker basket.

"Here's one thing more than you asked for," he said. They found room for them in the loft above the vegetable store. The Blue Checkers were the prettiest things about the place.

The sister in England did send a book, although it didn't arrive for almost a year. In any case, it only had one chapter of a practical nature. Otherwise, it was religious in tone. But meanwhile Kitty's calculations couldn't have been far off, because more or less when they expected it, the pains came on strong enough for Tanner to send for the doctor.

He had made the pigeons' nests out of packing cases. They ought to have flown out daily for exercise, but he hadn't been able to manage that. Still, they looked fair enough, a bit disheveled, but not so that you'd notice. It was four o'clock, breezy, but not windy. He took them out into the bright air which, even that far from the coast, was full of the salt of the ocean. How to toss a pigeon he had no idea. He opened the basket, and before he could think what to do next they were out and up into the blue. He watched in terror as, after reaching a certain height, they began turning round in tight circles as though puzzled or lost. Then, apparently sighting something on the horizon that they knew, they set off strongly towards Awanui. — Say twenty minutes for them to get to Parrish's loft. Ten minutes for Parrish or the Maori boy to walk up the street to the doctor's. Two and a half hours for the doctor to drive over, even allowing for his losing the way once. Thirty seconds for him to get down from his trap and open his bag.

At five o'clock Tanner went out to see to the pigs and hens. At six Kitty was no better and no worse. She lay there quietly, sweating from head to foot. "I can hear someone coming," she said. Not from Awanui, though, it was along the top road. Tanner thought it must be Brinkman. "Why, yes, it must be six months since he came," said Kitty, as though she were making conversation. Who else, after all, could it have been on the top road? The track up there had a deep, rounded gutter on each side which made it awkward to drive along. They could hear the screeching and rattling of his old buggy, two wheels in the gutter, two out. "He's stopped at the gully now to let his horse drink," said Kitty. "He'll have to let it walk the rest of the way." — "He'll have to turn round when he gets here and start right back," said Tanner.

There used to be a photograph of Brinkman somewhere, but Mr. Tanner didn't know what had become of it, and he believed it hadn't been a good likeness in any case. — Of course, in the circumstances, as he'd come eight miles over a rough road, he had to be asked to put up his horse for a while, and come in.

Like most people who live on their own, Brinkman continued with the course of his thoughts, which were more real to him than the outside world's commotion. Walking straight into the front room, he stopped before the piece of mirror glass tacked over the sink and looked fixedly into it.

"I'll tell you something, Tanner. I thought I caught sight of my first grey hairs this morning."

"I'm sorry to hear that."

Brinkman looked round. "I see the table isn't set."

"I don't want you to feel that you're not welcome," said Tanner, "but Kitty's not well. She told me to be sure that you came in and rested awhile, but she's not well. Truth is, she's in labor."

"Then she won't be cooking dinner this evening, then?"

"You mean you were counting on having it here?"

"My half-yearly dinner with you and Mrs. Tanner, yis, that's about it."

"What day is it, then?" asked Tanner, somewhat at random. It was almost too much for him at that moment to realize that Brinkman existed. He seemed like a stranger, perhaps from a foreign country, not understanding how ordinary things were done or said.

Brinkman made no attempt to leave, but said: "Last time I came here we started with canned toheroas. Your wife set them in front of me. I'm not sure that they had an entirely good effect on the intestines. Then we had fried eggs and excellent jellied beetroot, a choice between tea or Bovo, bread and butter and unlimited quantities of treacle. I have a note of all this in my daily journal. That's not to say, however, that I came over here simply to take dinner with you. It wasn't for the drive, either, although I'm always glad to have the opportunity of a change of scene and to read a little in Nature's book. No, I've come today, as I came formerly, for the sake of hearing a woman's voice."

Had Tanner noticed, he went on, that there were no native songbirds in the territory? At that moment there was a crying, or a calling, from the next room such as Tanner had never heard before, not in a shipwreck — and he had been in a wreck — not in a slaughterhouse.

"Don't put yourself out on my account," said Brinkman. "I'm going to sit here until you come back and have a quiet smoko."

The doctor drove up, bringing with him his wife's widowed sister, who lived with them and was a nurse, or had been a nurse. Tanner came out of the bedroom covered with blood, something like a butcher. He told the doctor he'd managed to deliver the child, a girl. In fact he'd wrapped it in a towel and tucked it up in the washbasket. The doctor took him back into the bedroom and made him sit down. The nurse put down the things she'd brought with her and looked round for the tea tin. Brinkman sat there, as solid as his chair. "You may be wondering who I am," he said. "I'm a neighbor, come over for dinner. I think of myself as one of the perpetually welcome." "Suit yourself," said the sister-in-law. The doctor emerged, moving rather faster than he usually did. "Please to go in there and wash the patient. I'm going to take a look at the afterbirth. The father put it out with the waste."

There Tanner had made his one oversight. It wasn't the afterbirth, it was a second daughter, smaller, but a twin. — But how come, if both of them were girls, that Mr. Tanner himself still had the name of Tanner? Well, the Tanners went on to have nine more children, some of them boys, and one of those boys was Mr. Tanner's father. That evening, when the doctor came in from the yard with the messy scrap, he squeezed it as though he were wringing it out to dry, and it opened its mouth and the colder air of the kitchen rushed in and she'd got her start in life. After that, the Tanners always had one of those tinplate mottoes hung up on the wall: *Throw Nothing Away*. You could get them then at the hardware store. — And this was the point that Mr. Tanner had been wanting to make all along: whereas the first daughter never got to be anything in particular, this second little girl grew up to be a lawyer with a firm in Wellington, and she did very well.

All the time Brinkman continued to sit there by the table and smoke his pipe. Two more women born into the world! It must have seemed to him that if this sort of thing went on, there should be a good chance, in the end, for him to acquire one for himself. Meanwhile, they would have to serve dinner sometime.

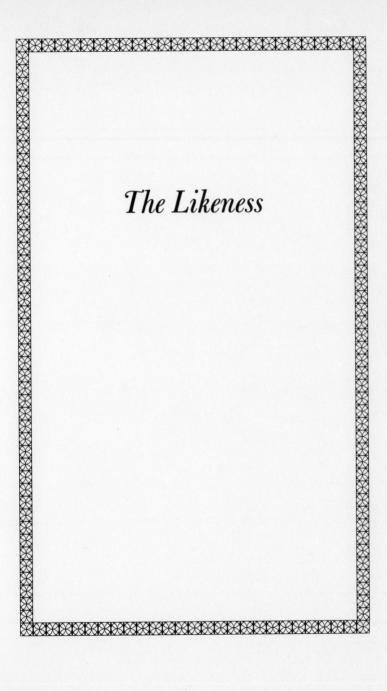

The Likeness

℘ MAKE NO MISTAKE, you pay for every drop of blood in your body.

Demetrius Christiaki was anxious, as far as possible, to please his father, who was a cotton importer, and still wore on his watch chain one of the gold 100 lira pieces which had been brought away out of Stamboul fifty years before when the family escaped to London. Father and son had had a number of disagreements, but not, fortunately, about Dimi's choice of career. He trained as an artist, in London with Luke Fildes, and in Paris with Gérôme. The Christiaki were prosperous but they were not materialists. In 1880, when Dimi was twenty, his father asked him to go to Stamboul to paint a portrait of his aunt.

Aunt Calliope (in reality the cousin of a great-aunt) belonged to a branch of the family which had chosen to stay behind in Turkey after the troubles. She lived alone, except for her servants and a great-niece, in the Greek district, the Phanar. She must be over seventy by this time, and was said to be in poor health. Dimi's father had a splendid collection of family portraits by Watts which he intended to leave to the South Kensington Museum, on condition that it should always be on show to the public, free of charge. It was almost complete; all the older generation were there save one — only Calliope was missing.

"I don't see why Watts refuses to go," said Dimi. "I believe he's in Venice."

"He hasn't refused, I haven't asked him. His digestion has become very weak, it would be madness for him to attempt the crossing."

"He gets a very good likeness."

"I have had you trained for three years," said his father. "Are you afraid?"

"Yes," said Dimi.

Christiaki Senior ignored this, and went on: "Good, well, I shall say nothing in my letter about either your drawing or your painting. You will explain my wishes in person. Go gently. Remember you will be in the Phanar, not in Alexandria."

"My aunt may not want me to paint her portrait."

"It will be your business to persuade her that you are competent."

"I meant that she might not welcome the whole idea."

"In any case, she will welcome a relative."

*

Dimi had not been to Stamboul since he was ten, a school-boy on holiday. Some things about it he could remember vividly, others not at all. The sober hush of the Phanar, terribly depressing to a ten-year-old, came back to him, and the relief of being taken out sailing almost as far as the mouth of the Black Sea. He recalled very clearly that in his aunt's house there was a well, or spring, which had been blessed four hundred years ago by St. Akakios the Harmless. At the time Dimi had drunk the water with reverence, confident that it would help him to pass his school tests.

He traveled by Messageries Maritimes via Marseilles and arrived just before nightfall, when the city which will last as long as there are men on earth looked its most enticing, not bettered by any engraving, its outline just at the point of disappearing into a pearl-grey sky. The Karaköy wharf, on the other hand, and even the Yeni mosque nearby, proved as the boat drew near to be black with smoke from the coal-burning ferries, while the water was crowded beyond belief with longshore traffic. Against the wooden piers of the Galata Bridge, filth and rubbish rode high. Shoals of fish, which had swarmed across to feed on human refuse, were hooked, gutted, fried and offered for sale in the cook-boats; consumers consumed.

Perhaps, Dimi thought, he ought to have traveled more respectably. But he was hardly established yet as a portrait painter, and it was a rule of the Christiaki that what you have not earned on your own account you must not spend.

If, when they were children, they were tipped sixpence or a shilling by some visiting man of business, they were required to give it back at once, with the explanation "I have done nothing that you should give me this." And if the kindly guest had turned away and was no longer listening, one had to tug at his sleeve and repeat the words louder. Surely no duty in later life could be more embarrassing than that. Dimi let his thoughts wander a little. He would arrive late, but he knew that there are moments when to keep count of time is to waste it. Halfway up the Golden Horn the ferryboat's engines faltered, and it had grown quite dark by the time the boat drifted, apparently at random, against the walls of the Phanar Iskelesi. High above him, and above the sea walls of the city, he could see the discreet lights of the Phanar.

Dimi's feet knew these streets. As he walked through the Petri carrying his one carpet bag, the high clouds drifted apart and showed him that the pavement widened a little to form a kind of square where two domed churches, sunken with age, faced one another. There was one light burning in the barred window of the night baker, who was preparing the church bread. Dimi turned a corner and went down three steps set at an angle to a blank doorway, deep in its stone recess.

Ten years ago a black woman who stood no nonsense had been on duty at the door. When he heard her voice at the grating he remembered her name, and said, "Ferahidil, it's Demetrius, Demetrius from England."

"Where is your servant?"

"I don't travel with a servant," he said. "I'm an artist."

One after another she drew back the bolts. As he crossed the forecourt behind her he could just see the reflections of her lamp in the gold of the icons and make out the position of the holy well. Ferahidil let him come only as far as the anteroom. Then she lit another lamp and left him alone while she fetched the coffee. This at least meant that he could consider himself received as a guest.

A young girl, however, came back with the silver tray, the two glasses of water, the two spoonfuls of jam. She was in Turkish dress, as though this—it was two o'clock in the morning—were a party, with bare feet in red leather isa-rouchia. To the exhausted Dimi her prettiness seemed an injustice. He knew it must be Cousin Evgenia. She must have been about five, as plain as a frog, and he had taught her, with the help of a few sweets from the bazaar, to count in English.

"Why aren't you in bed and asleep?" he asked.

"Tantine is in bed, I am staying up for you. Why didn't you come earlier? We sent a *hamal* down to Karaköy for your luggage. He has been there for two days."

"I haven't any luggage," Dimi said. "I hope he won't wait there much longer." First sitting upright on a chair, but then giving it up for a cushion, she chattered on in Greek,

Turkish, French and English without much distinction between them. She couldn't, however, quite get the English *j*, so that she spoke of jam as *zham*, and journey as *zhourney*. This was a relief to Dimi and enabled him, for the first time since he arrived, not to feel at a disadvantage.

Early the following morning he was called down to the salon to pay his respects to his aunt. This room again he half remembered. It was in the Turkish style, with six pairs of windows shedding their latticed cross lights onto the seats of honor at the far end. But the furniture was French, and sight was obstructed by an immense grand piano, made in Berlin and loaded down with Bohemian glass, piles of old journals and a bronze head of Gladstone by Alphonse Legros. Aunt Calliope, much smaller and thinner than he had expected, held out her hand to him from the "angle" beneath the right-hand window.

"Welcome, you have come."

"Welcome, I have found you," Dimi replied automatically, scarcely feeling that he spoke the truth, she looked so much worn away. She began to talk about his father, adding mildly, "Well, we are quite out of the world here. You have come from England to set us right."

"Why should you think that I want to do that?" Dimi cried in distress. "Do you think my father sent me over here to insult you?"

His aunt smiled. "You are shouting. What would your English friends say?"

Dimi paused. "They would say, 'Steady on, old fellow.'"

"Steady on, old fellow," she repeated in English, doubtfully.

With some idea of showing the worth or seriousness of his training he began to talk about the bust of Gladstone. He had met Legros often enough and could say that he knew him quite well.

"He lives in London, but he is French?" Aunt Calliope asked.

"Burgundian."

"Is it true that he can't read or write?"

"It may be true," said Dimi, "but there's no way of telling." He felt that he was losing her attention because he hadn't begun by saying something about the spiritual value of art. Everything in the room must have a higher importance for her, even the rubbish on top of the piano. Evidently she tired very easily. She told him that she regretted she would have to rest a good deal of the day, because old friends would be coming that evening for the express purpose of meeting him.

"Meanwhile, my dear, you have all you want. You are at home?"

Dimi considered. "Perhaps I'm not quite at ease yet. Last night, when I arrived, I was angry with myself because I thought my cousin ought still to be five years old."

"You don't want change?"

"I want progress, Tantine, certainly I do."

"Well," she said, "my Evgenia is still at school."

While his aunt had been speaking, Dimi had begun the study of her face from a professional point of view, calculating, as he had been taught, the primary, secondary and reflected lights. Her age could be indicated, he thought, without heavy shadows, simply by care with the flesh tones. But for some reason he did not like to suggest a preliminary sitting, not now, not yet. He might start by doing a few sketches from memory in his room, which overlooked the sea.

Ferahidil, with an attendant maid, came to take her mistress up to rest. At midday Evgenia returned — no longer, thank heavens, in fancy dress but in the uniform of her *gymnase,* with plain gold studs in her ears. The two of them sat down together at the low dining table, so that Dimi, who had been uneasily conscious of the heaps of scarcely worn red slippers in the corners of the room, waiting to be given to the poor, and each one lightly marked by her foot's impress, now found himself near enough to watch her breathing. The uniform confused him.

"Who are these people who are coming this evening?" he asked her. "Of course you must know them all."

"I know them." He thought she was going to go through the names, but she only said, "I hate them."

Dimi felt he couldn't let this pass, even if it was said for effect. "What have they done to offend you? Anyway, they will be guests in Tantine's house, and it's out of the question . . ."

It was not a success. At home he himself was the wild one, the bohemian. He had practice in ignoring reproofs, none in giving them. Evgenia gave him a bright glance.

"Steady on, old fellow."

"Where did you learn that?"

"I don't know. When I came back they were all saying it in the kitchen."

Since it was a fast day they were served with fish and a cheese dish. The flaky pastry was so light that it was difficult to manage — though not for Evgenia, who held her fork in her left hand but ate *alla turca* with two fingers and her right thumb. It was dexterous, but not quite civilized. He wished very much that he could make a drawing of her. That, however, would make her conceited, and it was not what he had come to Stamboul to do. Presently she threw down her fork and said, "Well, now you've come at last you can take me out into the city."

"Haven't you got afternoon classes?"

"Not now, not till later."

"But where do you want to go?"

"Anywhere. You can take me to church."

"Which church?"

"To St. Theodosia. There's a service of blessing there this afternoon for Professor Zographos."

"But I've no idea who he is."

"He died three years ago. When they last looked at the corpse it was not corrupted. The family are afraid that he is possessed by some other spirit."

"Professor Zographos was a teacher?"

"Yes, at the college."

"What did he teach?"

"Anatomy," said Evgenia absently.

"And what will they do if he holds up for another three years?"

"What would anyone do, cousin? Boil his bones clean."

She began to eat again and he turned the conversation to her studies. There was a new subject in the final year, psychology, but it did not interest her. Drawing, painting? No, she did none at all. But music she loved. Her piano was the only one in the Phanar, probably therefore the only one in Stamboul. When it was time for her to go to London, Dimi must take her to concerts; she had never heard an orchestra play. Dimi replied that he would be happy to take her to a Wagner concert and to present her to Mme. Wagner, whom he knew slightly. "Oh, cousin, yes, I beseech you . . ." She had turned pink, a pale rose color, delightful. So far, so good. No more on the subject of Professor Zographos.

But at that moment, something having been muttered by a servant as the glutinous desserts, powdered with fine sugar, were handed round, Evgenia declared that they ought to go out at once. Ferahidil wanted to fumigate the rooms on the ground floor. There was a hostile presence in the house. The servant, referring to it, had made the familiar sign to avert the evil eye. Ferahidil was never mistaken, it seemed.

"And what does she do?"

"She used to burn sage plant, to drive out the evil."

"And now?"

"Now we give her something modern, something from the English warehouse, Zheyes Fluid."

And this is my cousin, Dimi said aloud to the sea, the sky and the clouds, or rather this is my great-aunt's cousin's great-niece. Corpses possessed, the houses exorcised with Jeyes Fluid. This is the Phanar, I am a Greek, I am among Greeks, and yet I might as well be in Tibet.

He left Evgenia by herself to drink her coffee and crossed over on the next ferry to the Pera. At the end of the week his friends from London should be arriving — Haynes Williams, Philip Cassell and his sister Fanny, and Haynes's new wife, who was rather older than Haynes and would act, presumably, as a chaperone to the whole party. All four of them were artists; all of them intended to sketch picturesque oriental subjects. "We must meet your aunt," they had said. "We must meet this young cousin of yours. If you asked her, she might like to model for us."

"She mustn't feel afraid of us!" said Mrs. Haynes in a faint shriek.

Haynes wanted to have a go at the graveyard of Karaca Ahmet by moonlight. It would be a selling subject, he thought, for a steel engraving. Mrs. Haynes dressed rather smartly, which must cost him a good deal.

They had booked rooms in the Hotel Jockey, in a street just off the Grand' Rue. They would have preferred the

Phanar, so as to be as near to Dimi as possible, but in the Phanar there were no hotels. All who came there were Greeks, and every Greek could find a relation of some kind, however distant, to stay with. The Hotel Jockey, unfortunately, was quite without character. Dimi checked the price per night and per week. He told himself that he was looking forward to the arrival of his friends.

That evening the house still smelled a little of disinfectant, but it was splendidly lit, almost like his father's house in Holland Park. Evgenia took up her correct place in the anteroom, ready to help receive the guests. She was in white, which suited her less well than her Turkish outfit. She looked older, and wore European shoes.

As dusk fell a few elderly men — but each of them accompanied by more than one elderly lady, so that the salon soon filled — came in from the houses round about. Everyone talked about what had occupied them during the day, before the great city sank into the twilight of unsatisfied desires. The men, who had their little mannerisms, talked about profit and loss. The ladies surrounded Dimi, gently reminding him, or more often telling him for the first time, of family relationships. Only one guest circulated between the sexes. Perhaps, indeed, that was his function. He was apparently an indispensable man, prepared to laugh or be laughed at, just as the fish beneath the Galata Bridge were ready to eat or be eaten.

There were too many women at the soirée. It was interesting, however, to talk to old Mme. Sevastopolo, a relic, a skeleton, thinner even than Tantine, who when she had last been in London, as a child, had seen Byron's coffin passing through the streets. "The doctors killed the great poet," said Dimi. "That wouldn't happen now."

Mme. Sevastopolo looked at him in surprise. "Why not?"

While they stood talking Babikian began to flit from dish to dish, sampling a little of everything.

"He looks as though he had known what starvation is," said Dimi.

"Oh, I think you aren't right," Mme. Sevastopolo replied. "In my experience those who have starved are never greedy." And then, looking round the salon, "But where is Evgenia?"

"She left us quite a few minutes ago," said Babikian. "But Mr. Christiaki will be able to tell us exactly." Taking Dimi by the elbow, softly urging and squeezing, he persuaded him into one of the many little alcoves along the opposite side of the room. "How well do you know your cousin?" he asked.

"Not well at all," said Dimi. "She was a child when I last saw her."

"A touch of eccentricity there. So pretty, but perhaps even a little mad. But what would you say is the most noticeable change in her, beyond the development of the breasts? They, of course, are remarkable. I am speaking to you as an artist."

Dimi trembled. "I don't know whether you think I find you amusing, Babikian."

"Oh, you must call me Baby, otherwise people may think you take me seriously."

The soirée did not last long. By eleven o'clock there was a stir among the faded guests, who wished before they left to say goodnight to Evgenia, although they all lived in the Phanar and might expect to see her every day. Still she did not come, but Tantine made no apologies. The visitors' servants began to emerge from the kitchen to light their lanterns and dip their hands in the water of the holy well. Mme. Sevastopolo embraced Dimi and asked him, when he got back to London, to visit the graves of her relatives. "They are all interred at Shooter's Hill. Perhaps you know this hill?"

As soon as the last group of them moved away, still talking, the men's voices higher than the women's, Babikian a kind of *alto continuo* to be heard above the rest, the bright lights were all lowered, not for reasons of economy, but to return the house to its usual state of half-mourning, the seclusion of the Phanar.

The next day his aunt asked him whether it had crossed his mind that he might marry Evgenia.

Our Lives Are
Only Lent to Us

SC NONE OF THE native inhabitants of Santo Tomás de las Ollas saved any money and this was a moral imperative, although it worked differently from ours. We would think it a sign of respectability to "put by" now so as not to be an encumbrance to our relatives later. We wouldn't wish to be a burden to our folks. Mrs. Clancy put it this way at the get-together, the chicken-fry, which she, as the wife of the representative of the local manager of Providence Williams Marketing (Central American Division), gave from time to time to the American and European community; and in this she showed herself a sympathetic hostess because all the community were much occupied with assurance and its twin sister death, but the native inhabitants, although they too thought about death, had little interest in either saving or assurance. If they accumulated a little money by chance, they used it to employ a less fortunate member of their family to do something they found disagreeable and did not wish to do themselves. The benefit to their relatives came earlier but was not less welcome for that.

All this serves as an explanation of a visit Mrs. Sheridan paid one morning in October to her chauffeur, Pantaleón — or rather to his wife — for it was a visit of congratulation on the birth of a new baby. Mrs. Sheridan was the widow of a banker who had invested in silver mines (but the mines were nationalized now); her house, with faded shutters and faded pepper trees, was pointed out to strangers on the corner of the main square.

Pantaleón did not "live in" and was not required to work on saints' days, so that, as Mrs. Sheridan did not drive a car, it had taken some organization for her to make the call at all, since in Santo Tomás it was not possible to travel in a car some days and walk on others; you were either a walker or a driver and it would not have done to come to the *vivienda* in Calle López Mateos on foot. She had had to ask Mr. Azuela, an engineering executive with Mr. Clancy's firm, to call for her.

"Thank you, Don Salvador," she said as they arrived opposite the crumbling, well-like entrance.

"I'll stop by for you in ten minutes," said Mr. Azuela, always available, clever but difficult to like, with his gold teeth and blue suit, opening wide the car door.

Mrs. Sheridan walked steadily, not picking her way, out

of the entrance's shadow across the brilliant sun of the courtyard. Pantaleón's wife was not at the communal stone washtub and Pantaleón himself was not to be seen. Directed by enthusiastic neighbors, Mrs. Sheridan found him in the tiny inner patio, sunk in a basket chair, his face covered with soap. An elderly man was shaving him with a cutthroat razor.

"Don't get up, Pantaleón," she said, but he had done so already, knocking over the chair. His gentle Indian face under the mask of white suds creased with distress. Mrs. Sheridan shook hands with the elderly man, who wiped his hands on the seat of his trousers for the purpose — "my uncle" — and with two quarter cousins, not at all young, who had been cleaning respectively his right and left shoe.

"I am temporarily employing these people so that they can share in a little good fortune I have had," Pantaleón explained in his grave majestic voice. "It is not a matter of charity, of course. They are people of substance in their way. My uncle has a stall in the market."

Mrs. Sheridan knew that Pantaleón's wages were adequate and suppressed the thought that perhaps they were too generous.

"It was Rosario I really wanted to see, and your new son," she said.

"My wife is out shopping," Pantaleón replied.

"At the mercado, carrying a heavy basket! It's only ten days since the baby was born," protested Mrs. Sheridan.

"She is not at the mercado, she is at the supermercado. And my brother-in-law's niece is accompanying her to push the wire basket."

"And baby?"

"The baby is indoors with my little cousin — the great-niece of the señor uncle who is shaving me."

Mrs. Sheridan was used to the impact of the living room which, with its gleaming chromium bed, Virgin of Guadalupe framed in plastic lace, tall earthenware pitcher of water, sewing machine and worn stone grinder, showed the Indian genius for accepting from an overriding culture only what suited it best. In the rocker, with its cushion of embroidered electric-blue silk, sat a girl perhaps eight years old holding in her arms a baby wrapped in a shawl.

The Victorian novelists were right to make such children die; symbolically they were right since beauty of that kind is impossible in human beings beyond nine or ten. The girl's face had a golden waxy pallor and the modeling was so slight that there were hardly any shadows on it — even the lower eyelids made almost none. The round head was set with doll-like precision on the tiny neck that seemed ready to snap, and as it turned towards Mrs. Sheridan the pale and golden lights changed on the perfectly circular cheek. The child's golden stud earrings flashed and the very long eyelashes, which had a dusty or mealy look, opened slowly to contemplate the visitor.

"What is your name?" asked Mrs. Sheridan.

"Esperanza, señora."

"And you're Pantaleón's cousin? You're a relation of his?"

The child stood absolutely transfixed, turning on her a dark bright stare from the huge eyes of the undernourished. It was not an Indian stare — not blank, not withdrawn. Mrs. Sheridan, who had lived thirty-six years in Santo Tomás and was not a fool, recognized that she was treading on delicate ground, that of legitimacy.

"And where do you live?"

"In the mercado."

"But where do you sleep?"

"Under the stall. My great-uncle is from Chiapas, from the mountains. He doesn't like houses."

Esperanza traced something on the floor with her slender dirty foot — whitish, not blackish, with the eternal white dust of the mesa.

"But we are going to live here now, with cousin Pantaleón. He is paying to have mattresses made for us. They are being sewn now by his sister-in-law's great-aunt."

Mrs. Sheridan again felt surprised, and ashamed of her surprise.

"Will you like living here?" she asked.

"Yes, I shall like living with the baby. His life is my life."

She lifted a corner of the shawl and Mrs. Sheridan looked at the red-brown miniature face, still as an idol's. Now she was closer to the exquisite little girl, she noticed too an odor of fish and guessed what stall it was the great-uncle kept. The baby winked suddenly and blew a solitary shining bubble which broke without a sound.

"I do hope he's strong and healthy," said Mrs. Sheridan. The little girl carefully replaced the shawl.

"*Venimos prestados*," she said. "Our lives are only lent to us."

Colonel Terence lived at the Quinta María de los Desamparados, way above the town in its thick shelter of vines, chayotes, climbing pink geranium and organ-pipe cactus. The road out to it was a stony and featureless thirty kilometers and many of Mrs. Clancy's friends had said to her that it reminded them of the Holy Land, but once you were out there the Quinta, with its sounds of deeply moving foliage and falling water, was beautiful. It had seemed sad that all this might be largely wasted when the Colonel departed stateside for an operation for cancer of the throat, but now he was home again and, although he had not yet recovered his voice, he lay stretched out on the white wicker chaise longue well assured and insured, gentle, hospitable and long suffering.

"There isn't any skill a man can't master, once he's learned to discipline," said the new, youngish doctor. "That's where your army experience can't help but come in handy, Colonel. Now, this question of speaking without actually allowing the passage of air through the mouth —

well, people might think that'd rule out a lot of the vowels
and consonants altogether, but that's because they've never
orientated themselves to the idea of using the resonance
inside the mouth and chest. You take that talking bird,
Colonel."

The Colonel, caged in the white painted chair, looked
up to where his tame starling hung among the high flowers
and leaves of the first-floor balcony. The guests — Mr. and
Mrs. Clancy, Mr. Azuela, several of the business community — gazed up as he did to the lightly swinging cage.

"Salud, salud, salud," raved the high-hung starling; the
whole cage shook at the stream of pure liquid bubbling
sound. "Pretty Georgie Porgie, pretty pajarito, pretty boy.
My God, I can't bear it. My God, I must get out. My God,
I must go home. Pretty boy, salud, salud, salud. Estraight
home, salud."

"Plenty of people will tell you that a bird can't pro-
nounce those *s* sounds," continued the doctor, "but there's
proof positive that it can be done and you don't see that
bird's beak open a crack. The *st* sound it can't quite manage — not one Spanish native speaker in a hundred can say
that sound and not make it *est*, and you can't expect a bird
raised here to do any better."

They all watched and they did not see the bird's beak
open a crack. The doctor explained further and told them
— it was a semiformal gathering — that the Colonel needed
constant practice if his voice was to return at all.

"Georgie Porgie. Get out, you bitch," trilled the starling.

"I think I represent the feelings of the Colonel's circle of friends pretty closely," said Mr. Clancy at last, "when I say we are determined to see him through this thing and that we confidently expect that by Christmas he'll be a one-hundred-percent talking member of the community. We confidently expect that."

They faced the doctor with their good, unanimous eyes fastened on him and flashing through spectacles and contact lenses while above them the ragged mutterings of the starling died out in a long whirring trill, a clicking and whispering to itself and then silence. There was never quite silence, though, in the Quinta Terence, where there were so many movements in the spiked and creeping plants, servants shuffling across to throw water and sweep the patio five times a day, not bothering to pretend not to listen to what was said.

It was difficult to avoid the sensation of lecturing over the Colonel as if he were a lay figure. "It's a great relief to feel you're taking a hand in the treatment," the doctor said. "I want you always to let him take the initiative in a conversation. Don't start the talking—let him search for the words." The servants brought tequila, lime, salt and Montezuma beer, and the lay figure got up at last and poured and chinked the ice.

"It's certainly hard being called in at this late stage," added the doctor as they bumped away in his station wagon down the dry hillside. "Not that my predecessor didn't leave everything in order. I've formed the definite impression that the Colonel came here to escape from something. He's unfailingly kind and courteous but there's a difficulty in getting through . . . when I asked him to sign the forms before the operation . . . we simply ask routinely that all patients understand where our responsibility ends and theirs begins."

"You mean if they die, their responsibility would begin there," said Mr. Azuela.

"You're certainly wrong about the Colonel escaping," said Mrs. Clancy. "He was married when he came here and very proud to bring his bride to the Quinta. I mean she was quite young, and you have to consider that life can seem limited here. People can be homesick, and maybe feel trapped . . ."

"I'm just wondering how much more my tires will take," said the doctor. "This road's a killer. Do you know, it reminds me of the Holy Land?"

"We can't get close to them," said Mrs. Sheridan. "I've been living here thirty-six years and I feel I can't get in touch with them."

Since Mrs. Clancy was out, Mrs. Sheridan was received in the cool, double height drawing room by her niece, a serious, sweet-faced girl who had been training for a field trip with the Regional Centre for Fundamental Education.

"They told us at the Centre that responsibility for contact rested entirely with us, as we're guests in this country," the niece said. "You know we have six months theory and workshop practice before we go out to the mountain villages and they impressed on us that you could fail just as easily as you could succeed. You can go too fast speeding things up, like when one of our groups tried to get them to slap their tortillas twice with each hand instead of three times, but they didn't take into account that this three-time rhythm had a definite soothing effect. Or you can react and go the other way and feel that there's nothing to beat that cradle-to-the-grave pattern of peasant life and then you can't help them at all—you just get to be a cradle-to-the-graver yourself. Truly, although I'm not presuming to advise you, Mrs. Sheridan, it's just a question of study—you have to study the Indian mentality so you can understand where they can't be moved and where they're prepared to stretch a point."

"So you'll be going soon . . . to Oaxaca, is it?" said Mrs. Sheridan. "You must meet Colonel Terence first." She was truly interested in what Mrs. Clancy's niece was saying, but her mind seemed to drift across the high, shadowy ceiling, circling back always to its first point: I have been here thirty-six years and I am still no more than a guest.

"Pantaleón's father and mother came down from a mountain village," she added. "He's pure Indian, one supposes, but his little cousin didn't look like him at all. She reminded me of a wax doll or a golden doll."

As she left the house Mrs. Sheridan met Mr. Clancy rounding the corner of the *huerta;* he apologized for missing her in the usual half-shout which he used in the open air. The garden was beautifully kept, with thick tropical grass in which the paths seemed like partings and among the figs and bananas there were papery late roses, never quite fresh, never quite withered.

"You want to watch that Pantaleón of yours," said Mr. Clancy while they were still at a distance from the waiting car. "You may have noticed he's treating all his relatives lately; he's been shutting off the irrigation channels in your garden and diverting the water into his own patch; he's raising pumpkins and I daresay he reckons to make a killing on flowers for the Day of the Dead. No harm, I'd say, in having a word with him. The truth is, he's studied your mentality; he'd never take money but water's different; he knows where you can't be moved and where you're prepared to stretch a bit."

The mercado of Santo Tomás was not particularly old; neither was it picturesque. It was not visited by tourists nor by visiting experts from the Craft Section of the National Institute of Fine Arts. It had been erected, together with the little-used bullring, by a benefactor, a successful banderillero who had retired and died in his native town. It was a crazy structure of wood, a forest of rotting planks and struts, patched up with old doors from nearby building sites. The centre, where the meat and fish were sold, was to be avoided by all but the strongest-minded. The butchers hewed the carcasses as Samuel did Agag; they threw the entrails and the reproachful eyes behind the stall; a piece of meat in any shape was meat to the poorer customers. It was here that Esperanza and her great-uncle sold (when they could get them) fish and eels from the lake. Then came a wooden maze where fruit and sugar cane, aphrodisiacs, charms, spices and penicillin tablets were arranged in heaps on green leaves, and often sold by pinches or handfuls. The sweets stall was hopelessly outmoded, with a dusty showpiece of a hospital operating table, patient and surgeon all executed in sugar; there was a section for clothes and household goods and shoes soled with pieces of Dunlop tire — you could buy one shoe at a time in the mercado, or half a cigarette; and the whole thing petered out into a circumference of hopelessly ruined structures where old women offered oranges freshly cut and sprinkled with red pepper, or bootlaces and matches. Only the breadth of a street away glittered the supermercado, where everyone with the least pretensions to status or to spending money went to see and be seen. And yet the old mercado provided a precarious livelihood for perhaps a hundred people and gave many others a chance to scramble through on the right side of starvation.

Rosario, Pantaleón's wife, kept (sporadically, when she had the leisure) a toy stall with a stock-in-trade of pottery figures mixed up with plastic trash and objects filched from

corn-flake packets, while behind hung a selection of religious pictures: the guardian angel leading two children in
buttoned boots past a precipice, the Virgin of Guadalupe,
the Sacred Heart, all illuminated with gold and silver paper.
Only the pottery figures showed the native Mexican genius, the philosophy of the Toby jug, the gentle teasing of
the world, bringing it down to the scale of pitchers and
cups and household objects. There were whistles with
ears, pink horses and purple angels with stripes and flowers made into jugs with rough dabs of glaze. In the dark
recesses behind the shop were the obscene figures, combi-
nations of men and animals, which were bought by out-of-
towners on a spree.

"They're artists' work," said the sweet-faced niece, who,
unlike most visitors, had penetrated, escorted by Mr. Azuela,
into the dingy mercado. "It's delightful to think they make
them with such a sense of form and color for children to
play with."

"It is the children who make them here. Not the children
who play with them," replied Mr. Azuela. "Their fingers
are small and they learn early. Rosario's cousin, Esperanza,
makes these when she isn't selling fish or minding the
baby."

Rosario sat smiling broadly and peacefully.

"Let me purchase you something," said Mr. Azuela po-
litely. "A *cochinito*—a piggy bank. Perhaps this one with
purple roses."

"It doesn't seem economic only to have one opening," said the sweet-faced girl, turning the rough pottery pig over and over. "How would you get your money out again?"

"Only by breaking it, señorita," said Rosario decisively. "That is the *gracia* of the little pig. When you have saved you must break everything and spend everything. Then you can begin again."

The Colonel sat alone with the starling. He had had them lift its cage down and put it on the broad stone coping that ran round the patio. The bird was capricious. If anyone spoke to it, or if there was any noise about the place, it would listen intently, only moving slightly from one leg to another. Its favorite sounds were intermittent ones — hammering or sneezing, or the slapping of tortillas, or a pig being killed. Then, after about a quarter of an hour's silence it would wheeze like a mechanism about to strike and begin to talk, but the speech, as the doctor had said, was not outward-going but inward; its cheeks filled with air, its chest swelled, but its beak remained shut.

"I'm not going to be licked by a darned bird," thought Colonel Terence and, uncertainly and rustily at first, he began to follow it word by word:

"Salud, salud . . . pretty Joey — I want to get out of this place — estraight home . . . estraight home . . ."

Then he sank down sweating in the dark green shade of the vines. "I'll take a rest when the bird does," he thought.

*

Mrs. Sheridan did not really find it awkward to "speak" to Pantaleón; indeed, like an old married couple they could express many things without words, in a way which satisfied them both.

"Every man's obligation is to do what he can for his family," said Pantaleón with spacious gestures. "Nature and religion both demand this. The señora is aware that failure of the family hearth is the cause of many evils in this world. If men and women act without scruple it is because they have forgotten what God has made due to the family."

"All the same, I think you should cancel the order for the two extra mattresses. You might not find it possible to earn quite as much extra money in the future as you have done in the past."

It was just before Christmas when the old mercado caught fire. Earlier in the year, when the whole population was seated outside till late at night catching the cool air, someone would have noticed at once; that night, however, the first indication was the ruinous sound of cracking and snapping as the outer supports went. The actual smell of burning had gone unnoticed at first; few nights went by in Santo Tomás when someone did not set off firecrackers to celebrate something, even if it was only a win in the football pools, and the firecrackers were nearly always followed by scorching of some kind. But the bitter stench of burning wood grew stronger and then smoke rolled down some of the narrow streets which radiated from the market towards

the Plaza Mayor; almost in a moment it was mixed with the
more pungent smell of burning meat and fish.

Santo Tomás had no fire engine of its own. The only fire
engine had been adapted from a crop sprayer by Providence Williams; it was kept in the Clancys' carport along
with the Clancy cars and Mrs. Clancy's runabout. The pro-
vision of this public service helped to promote good relations between the Mexicans and Providence Williams,
and it demonstrated the benefits of efficiency since Mr.
Clancy's "team" of ambitious juniors kept it in good running order, thinking it was the old man's hobby. The crew
were volunteers from the town, but two of the Company's
staff had to be on board to drive and to direct operations,
and Mr. Clancy himself kept the ignition key.

"*El Señor Clancy no está.* This is Chela, the cook, speaking. The family are out."

"I must have him, woman. We need him. We need the
fire engine."

Chela could hear the sound of voices and the radio in
the background and knew that the *jefe* of police was speaking from the Café Central. The *jefe* was, in any case, her
cousin on her mother's side, Mrs. Clancy having been
shrewd enough to see the advantage of having a cook related to the police.

"It's you, Salvador. *Madre de Dios!* What's burning?"

"Where is he?"

"At the Quinta Terence. Ring him at the Colonel's."

*

Like wild animals from a cut cornfield, the stallholders whose only home was their unturned stalls staggered out of the burning market. They made gestures to show that others were still left inside. The patiently accumulated goods, the savings of a lifetime, were devoured one by one; the serapes, woven of raw sheep's wool with the oil left in it, blazed up with a suffocating smell of ancient sacrifice. The owners, weeping, dragged at the burning fragments. Meanwhile, people came running round corners and up the *callejuelas* as if blown from nowhere; Pantaleón was there among others, his mouth moving and his arms sweeping grandly, but anything he had to say was inaudible in that din. He was like one of the masked jumping figures in a fiesta, still in the white coat in which he had driven Mrs. Sheridan out to dinner. He was trying to explain about the question of the mattresses and about the relatives to whom, after all, he had not been able to offer the hospitality of his house. Someone handed him a bucket; they were filling them at the single cold tap on the patio of one of the *viviendas;* people were colliding with each other; the children darted between their legs and burned their fingers in the stream of brilliantly colored melted sweets.

"It's nice to see a wood fire," said the guests at Colonel Terence's. "If they stick to the new government regulations . . . if we're not allowed to cut down a single tree for firewood . . ."

"That's a problem I'm hoping to study at first hand,"

said the serious and sweet-faced girl, "up in the mountain villages. In spite of all that the commissions could do, I understand that currently they're still burning down trees to plant themselves another little patch of maize . . ."

"You will never go up to the mountain villages, señorita," said Mr. Azuela, flickering at her his gold teeth, his lizard eyes.

"Why ever not? What makes you say this?"

"You undertook this training for the best possible motive—because you have a pitiful heart. You pity those who need help, and in consequence you help those who need pity. You will find enough material here, I think, without making the journey to the mountains."

The telephone rang. It rang from the table beside the Colonel's chair, and with quiet deliberation Mr. Clancy leaned forward and held up his hand.

"No one will answer this telephone call for the Colonel," he said. "It can wait. We can all wait until such time as the Colonel can find words to answer it. I think we're all in danger of forgetting, in the enjoyment of our host's good food and wine—wish Chela could fix *huevos rancheros* like your cook does, Colonel—we're in danger of forgetting Dr. Smith's very explicit instructions about the recovery of your voice. I've noticed that you've spoken less than usual this evening. Now's your opportunity—don't force it, simply take your time while you search for the words."

But the Colonel must have been tired that evening, or

perhaps it wasn't one of his "nights," for his newfound skill seemed to have deserted him. Although he made a visible struggle, glancing out to the lighted patio where the bird-cage hung, the telephone rang on and on unanswered.

The new mercado at Santo Tomás de las Ollas was built as a spontaneous gesture by Providence Williams Marketing (Central American Division). It was designed by a modern architect with a German name from Mexico City, is made of reinforced concrete with murals of glass mosaic and is accepted, even by reactionaries, as a very real improvement. The funeral of Esperanza and her great-uncle was paid for by Mrs. Sheridan, who spared herself nothing, not even (under the firm guidance of Rosario) the most distressing details. There was no photograph available to put in the lace-framed holder on the white coffin, so the undertaker obligingly produced one from his reserve stock; it was of a blond, simpering little girl. "It is cute," said the undertaker. Thus even the image of Esperanza perished from the earth. The new fire station is at this moment under construction. The money is being raised by members of the American and European communities, a large donation having been given by Colonel Terence and the sweet-voiced Mrs. Terence.

Before the site was cleared, however, the old mercado rose for a short time a little way from its ashes. The poorest of the stallholders, to whom the loss of their tiny stock (nothing was insured) meant ruin, set up improvised fit-ups among the charred heaps of rubbish and tried to make enough to tide them over Christmas.

Mrs. Sheridan went down in honor bound to spend what she could. She was escorted — since Pantaleón's duties in the garden seemed to be more absorbing than ever — by Mr. Azuela.

"This question of the interaction of two cultures is not well understood," said Mr. Azuela, slowing down competently for the school crossing. "Some think that one will destroy the other, some think that the two will unite and create something new, as the Spanish civilization did with that of the Indian and the Jew. In my view, both are wrong. The two cultures are complementary, but in the way that death is to life. The two cannot exist together, but just as surely they cannot exist without each other."

Rosario was squatting broadly behind her stall, her head wrapped in her *tapabocas* against the morning air, which she thought it unhealthy to breathe. There was in fact a streaming white mist that morning which mingled with the smell of frying doughnuts and condensed on everything it touched. Rosario was offering for sale the clay figures for the Nacimiento — the Christmas crib. Whoever had made them, they were all there — angels, kings, peasants and knife grinders, shepherds and their strange-looking dogs, the Holy Innocents terribly streaked with bright red paint. Mrs. Sheridan smiled at Rosario, chose about a dozen figures and then hesitated.

"And the señora will buy the Holy Child?" Rosario asked with calm confidence. "Certainly you will want the Jesucristo."

"But it's so big, Rosario," cried Mrs. Sheridan, for the infant Jesus had clearly been salvaged from another set and was over a foot long. Made of rough earthenware, he towered over the delicate miniatures.

"What does it matter if he is big," said Rosario, wrapping up the figure swiftly in a piece of greyish-white paper. "After all, he is the king of the whole world."

Mrs. Sheridan looked round at the mercado, at the ruined black stumps of wood, which seemed bewildered, and the silent black stumps of old men and women.

"Oh, Rosario, I'm so sorry, so very sorry about everything!"

"You mustn't worry so much," said Rosario. "That is a fault. *Venimos prestados* — our lives are only lent to us."

A CHRONOLOGY

"The Axe." *The Times Anthology of Ghost Stories,* edited by Kingsley Amis, Patricia Highsmith, and Christopher Lee. London: Jonathan Cape, 1975.

"The Prescription." *The London Review of Books,* 1982.

"The Likeness." *Prize Writing: An Original Collection of Writings by Past Winners to Celebrate 21 Years of the Booker Prize,* edited by Martyn Goff. London: Hodder & Stoughton, 1989.

"At Hiruharama." *New Writing,* edited by Malcolm Bradbury and Judy Cooke. London: Minerva, 1992.

"Not Shown." *Daily Telegraph,* 1993.

"The Means of Escape." *Infidelity,* edited by Marsha Rowe (paperback original anthology). London: Chatto & Windus, 1993.

"Desideratus." *New Writing 6,* edited by A. S. Byatt and Peter Porter. London: Vintage/The British Council, 1997.

"Beehernz." *BBC Music Magazine,* October 1997.

"The Red-Haired Girl." *Times Literary Supplement,* September 11, 1998.

"Our Lives Are Only Lent to Us." Copyright © 2001 by the Estate of Penelope Fitzgerald.

Penelope Fitzgerald was born in Lincoln, England, in 1916. She won a scholarship to Oxford, where she studied with J.R.R. Tolkien and graduated with first-class honors in English literature in 1938. During World War II she was an assistant at the British Broadcasting Company and later worked at a bookstore and as a teacher of child actors. She was married and had three children.

Fitzgerald did not turn to writing until late in her life. Her first novel, *The Golden Child,* appeared in 1977 when Fitzgerald was sixty, launching an esteemed and prolific literary career. Her second novel, *The Bookshop* (1978), was a finalist for England's prestigious Booker Prize; she won the award in 1979 for her third novel, *Offshore.* Five more novels followed: *Human Voices* (1980), *At Freddie's* (1982), *Innocence* (1986), two Booker Prize finalists, *The Beginning of Spring* (1988) and *The Gate of Angels* (1990), and *The Blue Flower* (1997). She also wrote three biographies: *Edward Burne-Jones* (1975), *The Knox Brothers* (1977), a biography of her uncles and her father, editor of the literary magazine *Punch,* and *Charlotte Mew and Her Friends* (1984).

With the publication of her last novel, *The Blue Flower,* Fitzgerald won international acclaim and became a best-selling author. The book received the National Book Critics Circle Award in the United States and was an Editors' Choice of the *New York Times Book Review. The Means of Escape* collects her short stories for the first time. It was completed just before her death, on April 28, 2000, at the age of eighty-three. The paperback edition has been newly expanded to include two additional stories.

The novels of Penelope Fitzgerald
Available in paperback from Mariner Books

AT FREDDIE'S *"Occasionally one . . . knows by the bottom of page one that nothing but pleasure lies ahead. At Freddie's falls into that category."* — Listener. London's Temple Stage School, which prepares child actors for West End theater roles in everything from Shakespeare to musicals, is struggling against insolvency. In order to continue, the school's proprietress, Freddie Wentworth, brings anyone she encounters under her spell. Up to its surprising conclusion, *At Freddie's* is thoroughly beguiling. ISBN 0-395-95618-8

THE BEGINNING OF SPRING *"A marvelous novel . . . bristling with wry comedy."* — Newsday. In March 1913, the English printer Frank Reid returns to his Moscow home to find that his wife has abruptly gone away, leaving their three young children in his care. Shortlisted for the Booker Prize, this novel follows a rational man in a city where human experience — of love and friendship, of politics and power — is often unfathomable. ISBN 0-395-90871-X

THE BLUE FLOWER *"A masterpiece. How does she do it?"* — A. S. Byatt. Set in the age of Goethe, Fitzgerald's last novel tells the true story of the Romantic poet Novalis and his passion for a plain, simple child named Sophie von Kühn. A sublime meditation on the irrationality of love, *The Blue Flower* was awarded the 1998 National Book Critics Circle Award in fiction. ISBN 0-395-85997-2

THE BOOKSHOP *"A brilliant little book — no, it is perfect."* — Boston Sunday Globe. In 1959, Florence Green, a widow with a small inheritance, opens a bookshop in the seaside town of Hardborough. When her modest venture is met with polite but ruthless local opposition, her shop becomes a battleground. Shortlisted for the Booker Prize, *The Bookshop* is a classic comedy of stiff upper lip in the face of small-town nastiness. ISBN 0-395-86946-3

THE GATE OF ANGELS *"Vibrant with wonderful characters, ablaze with ideas."* — Washington Post. At Cambridge University in 1912, Fred Fairly, a rational young physicist, lives the life of a secular monk — until he meets Daisy, a working-class girl who changes his philosophy. As the *Daily Mail* said of this sparkling comedy, "Gilbert could have written it and Sullivan set it to music." *The Gate of Angels* was shortlisted for the Booker Prize. ISBN 0-395-84838-5

THE GOLDEN CHILD

"A classically plotted British mystery . . . leavened with a wicked sense of humor." — New York Times Book Review. When the ancient gold-covered corpse of an African ruler arrives at a London museum, it instantly becomes the sinister focus of a web of intrigue spun by all manner of museum personnel. Fitzgerald's unerring eye for the foibles of human nature, her humor, and her sense of the absurd are all wonderfully in evidence in this witty satire of the art world. ISBN 0-395-95619-6

HUMAN VOICES

"British writing at its best." — Boston Globe. The voices of this enchanting novel are those of an eccentric group of broadcasters at the BBC in London. During the air raids of World War II, the BBC has turned its concert hall into a dormitory for both sexes. And, as in any dormitory, romance and intrigue prevail. *Human Voices* is romantic, ironic, and tragic as only Fitzgerald can be. ISBN 0-395-95617-X

INNOCENCE

"The fullest and richest of all her novels." —Times Literary Supplement. The Ridolfi are a Florentine family of long lineage, eccentric habits, and little money. By 1955 the family, like its decrepit villa and farm, have seen better days. Only the youngest, eighteen-year-old Chiara, shows anything like vitality, but it's vitality matched by innocence — a dangerous combination, to herself and to all who love her. ISBN 0-395-90872-8

OFFSHORE

"Strong, supple, humane, ripe, generous, and graceful." — Sunday Times. On the Battersea Reach of the Thames, the slightly disreputable and the patently eccentric live on houseboats. There is Maurice, a homosexual prostitute; Richard, an ex-navy man; and Nenna, an abandoned wife with two little girls. Their story — a study in love and friendship among the temporarily lost — won Fitzgerald the Booker Prize in 1979. ISBN 0-395-47804-9